Celia Rees is a teacher and new writer. She studied
History and Politics at Warwick University and started
teaching history in 1973, but then changed to English. She
taught in comprehensive schools in Coventry for the next
sixteen years.

Her writing has the excitement and story-telling power
of the adult thriller but with teenagers as the central
characters. She says, 'There is no lack of subject matter:
murder, kidnap, abuse, runaways, bullying, rape . . . it is
all around, in every newspaper, happening to someone
every day.'

Every Step You Take was her first published novel for
teenagers, and is also available in Pan.

Celia Rees lives in Leamington Spa with her husband
and daughter.

Review of *Every Step You Take*

'An exciting blend of emotion and drama – not for the
faint-hearted!'

The School Librarian

Also by Celia Rees in Pan

Every Step You Take

And in Piper

The Bailey Game

Celia Rees

COLOUR
HER DEAD

PAN ORIGINAL
MACMILLAN
CHILDREN'S BOOKS

First published 1994 by Macmillan Children's Books

a division of Macmillan Publishers Limited
Cavaye Place London SW10 9PG
and Basingstoke

Associated companies throughout the world

ISBN 0–330–33512–X

1 3 5 7 9 8 6 4 2

A CIP catalogue record for this book is available from
the British Library

Phototypeset by Intype, London
Printed and bound in Great Britain by
Cox & Wyman Ltd, Reading, Berkshire

Chapter 1

The headlines had changed week by week, all through that so-called Summer of Love, charting the progress of the investigation.

First the tabloids had led with:

LOVE CHILD – HIPPY KILLING?

This had been followed by:

LOVE CHILD LATEST: YARD BROUGHT IN

And then, just when interest was dying down, one of the posh Sundays had come up with something new:

WHO KILLED LITTLE JENNY?
BERESFORD KILLING – MURDER BY WITCHCRAFT?

An enterprising reporter, sent to the area to research the case, had discovered certain odd coincidences and drawn some sinister conclusions. First, the murder date: the day after the summer solstice. Then the injuries that had led to death: a deep penetrating wound, piercing the heart, inflicted by a large, sharp, curved blade, possibly a sickle. Finally, another murder, still unsolved, had occurred in the area several decades before. Witchcraft was rumoured as the motive for that crime, too. The whole area was notorious for it.

Chief Inspector Jack Russell did not believe the witchcraft angle – never had. Initially he had regarded it as an

1

annoyance, a distraction, but it had seriously hampered the investigation. The witchcraft allegations cast a lurid glare over the whole case, attracting even more publicity, establishing the story in the public's mind, making it infamous. It still was. It had all happened so many years ago, but he still got letters asking for interviews. Even this week, two sixth formers from one of the local schools were supposed to be coming to see him about it.

No, it wasn't witchcraft, or anything like it, that had killed little Jenny. This was the product of a much more ordinary, everyday kind of evil. The case had never been solved. No one would probably ever know the true motive for the killing.

Motive dies in time, no matter how hideous the crime. Love, hate, lust, all crumble into the dust of memory. Even grief becomes assigned in the mind to some place less and less frequented. In the end only guilt remains, bright as metal on bone, fresh as the day it was minted.

He'd seen that, seen gold lockets gleam from below rotting throats, rings encircling skeletal fingers. The things he had seen. He passed a hand over his eyes as if to wipe away the memories. He'd thought, when he retired, to leave at least part of it behind. Some hope. His fingers returned to their aimless drumming on the arms of the chair. It was all there: the crimes, the faces, the bodies.

The clock on the mantelpiece whirred before beginning to strike the hour and somewhere upstairs a hoover droned. Mrs Stanley, doing the bedrooms. He'd told her not to bother. He only used one of them and what was a bit of dust? But she hadn't taken a blind bit of notice. She'd be down in a minute to make him a cup of tea. Ever since his daughter, Heather, had arranged for Mrs

2

Stanley to come in three times a week, he'd never drunk so much tea in his life. He was swilling with it.

"It's for the best, Dad. What with you having difficulty now, getting about, and us being where we are. If you insist on living here, I can't be coming back and forth all the time. It's hard enough getting away for the occasional visit."

She had adjusted her handbag on her knee and pursed her mouth. Heather was getting chins and middle-age spread, beginning to look just like her mother.

She had wanted him to move to sheltered accommodation near her but, when he agreed to a carer coming in, she had relented.

Carers. He didn't need carers. He could do for himself. He'd managed on his own for thirty years, ever since Sybil left him.

"You don't need me, Jack, and I've found someone who does."

His dead wife's voice sounded out of the past like a lost echo.

He took a gold half-hunter watch from his waistcoat pocket as the clock on the mantelpiece went through its sequence of chimes. The clock was a handsome piece. A brass plaque, screwed to the back, wished a happy retirement to Superintendent John (Jack) Russell, recording the gratitude of the communities he had sought to protect and the high esteem in which he was held after thirty-eight years in the police service.

Twenty years. It would be twenty years since he retired, come this summer. His head shook slightly, an old man's tremor. He couldn't believe it. He hadn't wanted to go, hadn't wanted to leave, not with his case load uncleared, files still open. Jack Russell always gets his man; he'd been

3

famous for it. But the regulations were clear. Statutory retirement age, you had to go when you reached it.

He remembered the little speech he'd made, before they swapped polite sherries for doubles in the pub. He'd told them about his chosen place of retirement. A cottage hard on the wooded slopes of Mitre Hill in the village of Coombe Ashleigh. He'd made no mention of the Beresford case, but the Chief Constable's eyebrows had shot up and some of the younger ones had grinned and winked: you had to hand it to the boss, he never gave up on anything. Other colleagues had registered concern, even distaste: that bloody case again, old Jack had become totally obsessed by it.

The Beresford child. In the file she was Jennifer Anne; to the press Little Jenny. Just six years old, her birthday had been a couple of days before. She had gone with her mother to the local fête and, on that bright June afternoon in 1968, she had disappeared. Two days later her body had been discovered, buried up on Mitre Hill, high above Coombe Ashleigh village.

Returning his watch to his waistcoat pocket, Jack groped for a moment, feeling for the small object he always carried there. He did not need to see it, his fingers held the memory of its curious lozenge shape and ornate embossed pattern. A green glass bead. Unusual, distinctive, it came from the necklace the child had been wearing at the time she disappeared. The beads had left their mark on the little girl's neck. The one in his hand had been discovered with others, scattered across the site of the murder. The rest of them had never been found, neither had the killer.

*

Jack and his team from County CID were brought in after the discovery of the body. They should have been summoned sooner; the search parties and the local bobbies had tracked everywhere, muddying the whole site, and someone had moved the body. It was a hot day, the shirt covering her was circled with sweat at each armpit. Jack had been told how she had appeared to have died, slaughtered like a young calf, sliced through the back with a sickle or a scythe. For the moment, he preferred to leave the covering over the body.

Her feet stuck out, white socks, no shoes. He looked round, testing the ground. Wet underfoot, squelchy. There had been thunderstorms for two nights, yet her feet were bone dry. They weren't at the killing site. He lifted the cover and stood looking down at her. Someone had closed her eyes. Just looking at her face reminded him of his own daughter asleep. But then his nose caught the slight, sickly scent of decay and he saw the streaking and heavy staining on the rest of her body.

A chain of small bruises round the throat. Someone had tried to strangle her first, before doing the other thing. He moved her head. The long fair hair was matted with earth and leaves. Faint flower patterns, big and daisy shaped, could be discerned under the dirt on both her cheeks. The word LOVE showed faintly, written across her forehead. He'd bent closer, going down on one knee; it looked like some sort of grease paint, or it might be lipstick.

Someone leaked this detail to the press, that was how it came to be called "The Love Child Killing". The headlines continued, monitoring the frustrating lack of progress that dogged the investigation.

*

He reviewed the case again as he had innumerable times. They had been thorough, meticulous. Hundreds interviewed, the investigation had taken them all over the country, but one by one every lead dried up.

They were left back here: the village where it had all started. And this was where it would finish, there was still no doubt in his mind. A local had killed her, someone known to the child, someone from Coombe Ashleigh, and that individual was being shielded.

They still might have got somewhere if it had not been for that article in the *Sunday Times*. At the mention of witchcraft the village had completely clammed up.

"Stranger. Had to be," was all they had ever said about it.

Visitors, hippies, they had all sorts of theories about outsiders of every kind, but enquiries about any of their number had been met with sullen silence. Never, in all his years in the Force, had he come across such lack of co-operation. It still baffled and angered him. Sometimes he thought the whole bloody village was banding together to protect whoever did it.

"Can't arrest without proof, Jack. Can't move on hunches." Chief Superintendent Lineham had said as he prepared to return to Scotland Yard. "And at the moment we've got sweet FA, not even a suspect. I'll be back if anything breaks, but meantime – go easy on the conspiracy theories."

There had been no breaks, no new evidence. DCS Lineham had never come back, he had gone on with his successful career with the Met., putting the Coombe Ashleigh murder behind him. No unsolved case file was ever closed, but this one was history now, for everyone. Except Jack Russell. He didn't need a file, it was all in his head.

And on his conscience. The Beresford case had smirched his career record and shadowed his retirement.

He'd long ago given up any ambitions he might have harboured about solving the case. But all these years he'd clung to the hope that he could somehow strip away the cloak of innocence and expose the guilty one by his very presence.

Someone knew who'd killed that little girl, and they were still protecting the bastard. He couldn't stand the thought of them resting easy, thinking they'd got away with it. He was a reminder. Lest they forget. A child's life had been taken. Justice had yet to be done. And a killer remains a killer, whoever they might appear to be on the surface.

Jack Russell took out his watch again: must be nearly dinnertime. He watched the hand sweep round the last second of his life and then his vision blurred as the blood boomed in his head.

"Massive stroke, the doctor said," Mrs Stanley later told the village. "Of course, I was the one that found him. Must have gone just like that," she added, clicking her fingers for emphasis. "Must be the time of year. Midwinter carries 'em off like nobody's business."

Chapter 2

Jack Russell's funeral had come and gone. The February gales had blown themselves out and, although it was still cold, there were definite signs that spring was on its way. Pussy willow and catkins, Jude Hughes had noticed them in the hedgerows on the route into town. It was Saturday morning and she was well into her round of charity, junk, and antique shops. In the summer the town's beautiful river side-setting, its picturesque buildings and long history, attracted huge numbers of tourists; but on a chilly day in early March the narrow streets were mercifully less than crowded.

She had come on the bus with Emma but as usual they had split up. Emma always went straight to the new shops, built in a system of arcades and alleyways behind the old half-timbered buildings. Or she would be in the mall, striding across the grey marble floors, gliding up and down on the escalator, mentally ticking off her shopping list: Our Price, Monsoon, Body Shop, Miss Selfridge.

Emma was Jude's best friend. They agreed on a lot of things, but when it came to shopping for clothes they definitely parted company. Everything Jude had on was second-hand, barring her socks and underwear. But the old clothes smell in Oxfam made Emma gag and she could not see why anyone wanted anything if someone else had owned it. She always knew what she wanted and went straight to it. Jude, on the other hand, never even knew what she was looking for until she had found it.

Jude was staring into Cooper's Antique Market. She had saved it until last. A lot of the stock was way beyond her means but they always had a refreshing leavening of genuine junk among the antiques and in the past she had found some great bargains. She peered through the dusty over-stuffed window pretending to see if there was anything new, but she was really looking to see if Ben Cooper was there. He sometimes helped his dad on Saturday mornings.

She had fancied Ben for a long time and, recently, at a couple of parties and the odd disco, she had thought he might be feeling the same about her. The last time had been most promising. They had danced together all night and he had taken her home. It could be the start of something.

The bell tinged loudly when she opened the door. Jude glanced around, checking herself quickly in the long mirror propped against a worn sideboard. She pushed a hand through her thick golden hair and shook it out over the shoulders of her battered leather jacket.

There was no one behind the counter, no sign of Ben or his dad, only one or two browsers. Her face in the foxed mirror registered disappointment. She walked past an old juke-box, which had been put with the collection of one-armed bandits and fairground machines, to the bric-à-brac shelves at the back of the shop. Her boot heels on the bare wooden floor sounded like mocking laughter.

She combed her long fingers through and through the mound of buttons which filled a large cracked mixing bowl. To Emma, buttons were buttons. She had never sewn one on anything in her life, but if the need arose they could be purchased in Woolworths. Emma would find these, snipped from people's lives, less than fascinating. Workaday ones – plastic, wood, mother-of-pearl – were mixed up with bright glass, crystal cut or smooth as sucked sweets, sometimes even jet or diamanté. Jude's fingers found something and she shook it out. Three shirt buttons on a piece of card, she held them for a moment – Warden's, High Street, 1/6, a fragment of time – and then dropped them back to resume her searching.

Her hand stopped and she forgot about Emma and Ben and everything else. She took something out of the pile and went to where there was more light. This wasn't a button, it was a bead. She examined it carefully, turning it round and round. It looked old and handmade. It was oval, about two centimetres long, a lozenge shape of swirled milky-green glass. On the surface a delicate pattern stood out in relief. A fragile tracery painted in gilt wound round crimson buds like tiny beads of blood and in and out of pale blue flowers and pink roses. It was lovely.

She went back to the buttons, maybe there were more. Her search was painstaking and systematic. This was quite a find and – she checked the felt-tipped price taped to the bowl – at 20p for ten, it could amount to one of her best-ever bargains. She found another, then another, and placed them carefully next to each other, until they formed a little row on the shelf beside her. She looked round guardedly now and again in case anyone realized she was on to a good thing and came to see what she was doing.

It was not until she was entirely sure the bowl contained no more that she stood back to count them. Nine altogether, not bad, not bad at all. She smiled to herself, already seeing in her mind the necklace she was going to make. She had all the beads now, just had to go to the craft shop and get some fixings.

Somewhere behind her the juke-box clicked and whirred into life. The song boomed out all around. She turned immediately, jolted by the opening chords. It always seemed as though the singer was calling "Hey Jude" to her personally.

Her heart gave another jolt when she saw him there, standing with his arms folded, back against the counter, miming the words to her. When her dad did that it made her furious, but now she found herself blushing, feeling idiotically pleased and special. He had noticed her, and he had thought about her, at least for the time it took to go and punch in a song.

Ben Cooper forgot to mime the rest of the words and started to laugh at the impact the Beatles' tune had made. Shock and surprise had given way to confusion in her face. He'd never seen Jude Hughes so disconcerted. As he came over, his teasing grin turned to a genuine smile.

"Hey, Jude . . ."

"Don't start again!"

"OK, OK. I just couldn't resist it. Great juke-box. Genuine sixties classic." He gestured over to the big squat machine. "Came in last week, works on old ten ps, still got loads of the original forty-fives on it. What are you looking for? Find anything interesting?"

Jude had almost forgotten the beads. She turned to pick them up.

"Found these, in with the buttons."

He took one from her and examined it carefully.

"Umm," he said. "Looks old. Kind of art nouveau,

11

could be Edwardian or even later Victorian . . . How many have you got?"

"Nine – with that one."

He handed the bead back and looked at her, head on one side. "Tell you what. I'll let you have them for, say . . ."

"Twenty p," Jude said firmly, pointing to the price on the bowl. "Try to charge me more and I'll have you under the Trade Description Act."

"But these aren't buttons!"

"So? Twenty p for ten it says. It doesn't specify buttons."

He laughed. "Just kidding. Let's see your money then."

She handed him a twenty-pence piece.

"Hold on," he said, "you're one short."

He took a button from the bowl and held it up next to her head.

"This'll do," he said, spinning and catching it before presenting it to her. "Matches your eyes."

Her hand closed over the button. Flower shaped, cornflower blue, almost violet, it was a beautiful colour.

"Thank you," she said, glancing away, embarrassed.

"Hey, Ben – get over here. You're supposed to be helping me. I'm not paying you to chat up girls – even ones as pretty as she is."

His father, a big, thickset man in filthy blue overalls and an old pullover full of holes, dropped the dining-room chairs he had just carried in through the door and went out to the van for another lot.

Ben held the door as his father staggered back in under a small chest of drawers.

"Any more?" he asked, peering out at the street.

"Stevie can do the rest this afternoon," his father said,

wiping the sweat from his forehead. "I'm going for a pint. You coming?"

"Well, er . . ." Ben started as Jude came up.

"Bring her as well. Over the Queen's Head. Lock up, will you? I'm just going to the van to get my jacket."

Ben flipped the "closed" sign over and ushered the few remaining customers out. On the juke-box, the last chorus of the Beatles' song faded away as he pulled the door shut and locked it.

"Fancy a drink?" he asked.

Jude bit her lip, looking at her watch. "Well, I shouldn't really . . ."

"Oh, come on – one won't hurt." He smiled down at her and took her arm, making her mind up for her.

She was supposed to meet Emma but that wasn't for nearly half an hour. There was plenty of time. Emma wouldn't mind waiting for a bit. She'd understand. This was an opportunity not to be missed.

Chapter 3

Jude was nearly three-quarters of an hour late in the end and Emma did mind, she minded a lot. She leapt to her feet as soon as she saw her and marched up, furious.

"Where have you been?" she demanded. "I've been waiting ages and it's freezing. One more minute. One more minute, Jude, and I was leaving . . ."

"Look, I'm really sorry—"

"You've been drinking!" Emma leant close, sniffing suspiciously. "I've been getting hypothermia waiting for you and you've been sitting in a pub somewhere. Terrific!"

"I only had two halves of cider . . ."

"Cider!" Emma's nose wrinkled. "How could you drink that? It's disgusting!"

"Ben's dad bought it for me."

"Sorry? Who? Whose Dad?"

"Ben. Ben Cooper."

"OK – let me get this straight. I've been waiting three-quarters of an hour for somebody I thought was my friend while that person was in a pub with Ben Cooper's dad – is that right?"

"Ben was there too," Jude added.

"Oh," Emma gave a sarcastic smile, "I see! Ben was there too! Punctuality, loyalty, friendship," she shrugged, "all nothing compared with a chance to touch knees with the gorgeous Ben Cooper."

Jude grinned.

"Sorry," she said, "come on – I'll buy you a coffee."

Emma refused to budge. "I can't be bought off that easily."

"OK. How about hot chocolate with whipped cream and one of those almond croissant things?"

"Umm," Emma pretended to consider for a moment. "All right. Let's go."

Jude stirred her cappuccino and watched her friend tear into the croissant, scattering almonds and icing sugar all over the table, greedy as a child. Sometimes Emma wore her carefully cultivated sophistication very lightly. She would never drink cider in a pub, always Perrier spritzer or vodka and tonic, but she had a huge appetite for sweet things, marshmallows, popcorn at the cinema, pick'n'mix. And she was one of those slim people who seemed to be able to eat anything without ever putting on weight.

"What are you thinking?" Emma asked as she picked up the last few flakes of almond on the end of a moistened finger. A faint crusting of sugar had added itself to the cream moustache left by the chocolate.

"I was just thinking how greedy you were. Here," Jude handed her a paper napkin, "for God's sake wipe your mouth."

"Those are really good." Emma indicated the wreckage on the table and tossed the crushed napkin, stained crimson by her lipstick, on to the plate. "You should have had one."

Jude shrugged. "I wasn't hungry."

"In love, eh?" Emma brushed the crumbs off her long black coat and black jeans with her purple scarf.

"Oh, don't be ridiculous!"

Jude could feel her patience stretch. She'd made no secret about her liking for Ben Cooper but she was not going to put up with endless teasing about it.

"Did you get anything?" Emma said, sensing her friend's tightening mood and changing the subject. "Apart from a cider with beautiful Benjamin?"

"Yes, actually," Jude replied, ignoring the last dig.

"What?" Emma looked under the table for packages. "Not more disgusting second-hand garments, I hope. That waistcoat you got last week looked like someone had puked down it."

"That reminds me, I've got to pick it up from the dry-cleaners, and I want to go back to the craft shop because I found these."

Jude felt in the pocket of her leather jacket and brought out the beads.

"How many are there?" Emma asked, as Jude put them in a little group on an unused napkin.

"Nine." She sorted them carefully into a row. "They all come from the same necklace. I'm going to restring them with some I got from that new bead place. What do you think?"

Emma picked one up and looked at it. Jude's face was faintly flushed and excited, her blue eyes distant, already seeing the finished necklace.

"They're really pretty," she said, "unusual. I've never seen any quite like them. Should be good." She touched the moonstone ear-rings Jude had given her for Christmas. Some of the things she made were beautiful. "Where did you get them?"

"Ben's shop. All mixed in with buttons. Ben's dad reckons they might be worth quite a lot but they had to let me have them for twenty p – a real bargain!"

16

"Plus a drink with the man of your dreams. You have had a successful morning." Her friend leant forward. "Come on, Jude. Tell Emma. What did you talk about?"

"Well," Jude's face clouded over, "nothing much really. Ben's dad did most of the talking. They'd been out doing a house clearance and – and d'you know whose it was? Jack Russell's."

Emma frowned and shook her head. "Real bummer that happening, Jude. Blew a hole right through the project."

"God, Emma. Sometimes you are so insensitive. It must be terrible to die like that, all alone and friendless."

"He wasn't alone. Mrs Stanley was there. Don't be so melodramatic."

"She wasn't exactly a friend, though, was she? And you said yourself, everyone in the village resented him being there."

"It was his choice. He chose to live there and everyone knew why. Of course they are going to resent it."

"Even his daughter couldn't care less, Ben's dad said, she didn't want a thing – getting rid of the lot."

Emma shrugged. "That's families. Come on, let's go." The place was getting crowded now and two women with trays and toddlers in tow were hovering by their table, staring pointedly at them. "I want to go to Smiths and then it's dry-cleaners, craft shop and home. On the way," she linked Jude's arm, "you're going to tell me all about you and Ben Cooper."

It was Jude's turn to pay their bus fare and all she had was a note. She collected her change and made her way to the back, past the scattering of other passengers. Emma was already engrossed in her copy of *Elle*, as Jude slid into the seat next to her and didn't seem too inclined towards conversation, so Jude braced her legs against the seat in front and gazed out of the grimy window as the single-decker juddered and shook, nosing its way through the congested town streets, heading for the dual carriageway.

The road was relatively new and had been built on a slight ridge, designed to take passing traffic above and around the small villages and their connecting web of narrow country lanes. Jude liked this particular bus route. You could see a long way from up here. It gave you a different view. She leant her head against the window, looking out for landmarks.

Far, far to the left was Mitre Hill. It was the tallest in a chain of hills which marked the edge of the flat lowland plain and its shape was unmistakable, even from this distance, its shoulders cloaked with trees. It didn't look particularly sinister, even in the failing light of oncoming night, but there were lots of stories and superstitions associated with it and some people wouldn't walk on Mitre Hill, even in the daytime.

The village of Coombe Ashleigh, where Jude now lived in what had been the schoolmaster's cottage, nestled at its base and looked out at a flat chequer-board landscape: patches of dark woodland alternating with hedge-fringed green fields. Hill Ashleigh lay just behind the ridge. It was different up there; unfenced rolling country. Hill Ashleigh, that's where Ben came from. Jude's mind suddenly jumped to wondering if he would be on the bus on Monday, if he would talk to her, come and sit by her.

"Penny for them."

Jude turned to her friend, suddenly aware that Emma

18

was watching her. She could not admit she'd been day-dreaming about Ben, Emma would only start teasing her again. Instead she said:

"I was just thinking about our project and, you know, the Beresford case."

Emma followed her gaze. Mitre Hill was nearer now, looming dark against the sky. Its features became indistinct even as they watched. Up on the hill it was night already. Something about that place, the notorious case, the fact that it had happened where they lived, where Emma had grown up, fascinated both of them. It was not clear who had thought of it first, but a plan had been hatching for some time to submit it as their local history field-work project.

"Have you spoken to Conrad about it yet?"

"Well, no . . ."

Emma groaned. "I thought you had! The proposals were supposed to be in to Wyatt ages ago."

"Like you said, Jack Russell dying like that, kind of put us back. I'll write it over the weekend. It might be a bit late but Clare won't mind."

Emma and Jude were in different sets for History. Emma had Mr Wyatt, the Head of Department, while Jude was taught by Clare Conrad who was not just more interesting and more attractive, but was also much more understanding as far as deadlines were concerned.

"Still got to get it past Wyatt," Emma pointed out.

"So? What can he object to? It'll be original research! There's loads of archive material, like newspapers and stuff, and we are going to interview people who remember it. People in the village – like Mrs Stanley. She knows everything that's happened in the last hundred years."

Jude laughed. "We could even tap Wyatt himself, he comes from the village."

Something told Emma that might not be such a good idea. She stared at her own reflection, as the darkness outside made the window into a mirror.

"What's the matter?" Jude asked after a moment or two.

"Nothing. I'm just worried he might not go for it."

"Is that all?"

"Yes."

"Are you sure?"

Emma nodded.

"Frankly, I don't care. I'm going to do it anyway."

"And that's that?" Emma smiled.

"Yeah," Jude grinned. "That's that."

Jude took ages to decide things and usually did so by a roundabout route of signs and portents but once she had made her mind up, she could be surprisingly stubborn. Although Jude had only lived in the village a short time, she was the best friend Emma had ever had, the only real friend to be honest; Emma did not make friends easily. And this was a good idea. It fitted the brief for the local history assignment like a glove. Even so, part of her wished this project had died with Jack Russell. She bit her lip and glanced back at her friend. They had not really discussed this enough. Emma had lived in the village all her life and knew things that Jude did not. It could be unwise, dangerous even, to stir things up. It felt like they might be taking a big risk. To Coombe Ashleigh, some things were still not history.

Chapter 4

Tuesday morning marked the second day that David Wyatt, head of History, had been unable to get any further than a street of terraced houses adjacent to the sixth form annexe. If he wound his car window down and listened carefully, he could hear the bells announce the beginning and then the end of lessons. But he sat, windows closed, staring straight in front of him.

He smoothed his thinning red hair and removed his gold-rimmed glasses. The bridge left deep indentations on either side of his bony nose. His eyes felt hot, the skin around them papery and thin. He had the most ferocious headache. He glanced up at the mirror, glad of the blurring caused by his myopia. Even to himself he looked strange now without his glasses. He massaged his jaw line, the flesh felt loose and was patched with stubble. His skin was an unhealthy grey except for the high colour on the cheeks and nose brought on by last night's drinking.

You can't go on like this. He stared into the eyes in the mirror. Mum's death was a shock, yes, but it wasn't unexpected. You've got a job, children, a wife. You've got to get your life together.

So far his wife, Elizabeth, had been quite considerate and reasonable, but even in his present state of self-absorbed distraction he could detect that her patience was frayed to the edge of breaking. Time heals, they say, so it should be getting better now. He closed his eyes and rested his head on the steering-wheel rim. But it wasn't. Every day it just seemed to get worse and worse.

After the bell signalled the start of morning break, Clare Conrad headed for the students' common room looking for Jude Hughes. She struggled through the door into wraparound sound; the stereo system only allowed for shouted conversation. The Principal's choice of bright modern furnishings was not standing up very well to the pounding it took and every available surface was littered with plastic cups, empty wrappers and other debris, the remains of refreshments served by the battery of vending machines that stood against the far wall.

She couldn't see Jude anywhere, but she spotted the sweep of shiny magenta hair being thrown back, and a flash of dark red lipstick, as Emma Tasker turned to smile at something someone said.

"Emma, do you know where Jude is?" she shouted, enunciating carefully. It was like trying to talk in a disco.

"No, sorry," Emma mouthed, shaking her head.

Clare held up a clear plastic wallet. It contained Jude's proposal for the local history project.

"I want to see her about this."

Just then the stereo went off and, in the silence, Clare's voice boomed round the room.

"That always happens to me," she said, dropping her voice to normal.

"Me, too." Emma laughed. "It should be quieter for a bit while they all squabble about what to put on next." She pointed to the folder. "What did you think?"

"It's a really good idea . . ." Clare said, but her face and her voice expressed the same doubts Emma had felt on Saturday night, "and it would make an interesting study. But I need to see her about it."

"Is Wyatt – Mr Wyatt in today?" Emma asked.

The teacher shook her head. "He's off sick."

She nearly added "again" but that would have been unprofessional. Still, it was happening a lot now and it was beginning to really rankle. No one had grudged Dave the time when his mother died, but that was months ago. He couldn't keep having time off, leaving her to do all the work. At the end of the month he was the one taking home the Head of Department's salary.

"Who's taking us then?"

"No one. Fieldwork. That's why I need to see Jude. I thought we could all go down to the library and get started on these projects."

Emma's reply was lost in the sudden rush of music.

Clare Conrad shouted something else but Emma shook her head. The teacher motioned towards the door. This was hopeless.

"Are you OK for photography later?" she said when they got outside.

Emma had joined the photography group because she wanted a career in journalism and it seemed like a relevant thing to do, but now she was genuinely hooked and was getting to be good at it.

"I don't know," she said, shaking her head. "I haven't got a lift tonight and if I miss the bus I've had it."

"I'll give you a lift." The teacher smiled. "I'm going out your way to see my dad. I was going to drop in on your mum too, so you've got no excuses. Anyway I thought they wanted you for that tableau thing."

Emma smiled back. She had fine eyes, large and dark, in a face that was all planes and angles. Her looks were

23

unusual, hovering between ugliness and beauty, but the camera loved her, she was very photogenic. Her short hair was always immaculately cut and the colour had changed yet again, the natural mid-brown dyed to a deep mahogany, almost purple, hue. If she wanted to, Clare thought, she could make her career in front of the camera rather than behind it.

"Oh," she said suddenly, "I've got something for you. Hang on, it's in here somewhere. I found it in one of the Sunday papers."

She rummaged through her briefcase and brought out the cutting she had taken.

"It's a journalism competition, entrants from sixteen to twenty-something. Thought about you as soon as I saw it."

Emma took the competition details from her. Last year her two weeks' work experience had been in the offices of the local newspaper. As soon as she walked through the door, she knew. She wanted to be a journalist.

Everyone kept pointing out how competitive it was, how difficult it would be to get a job, but Emma was not deterred easily. She'd worked on the paper in the holidays, and was assistant editor of the school magazine. Now this. It would look good, very good indeed if she could win a national competition.

"Thanks, Clare," she said, tucking the cutting into her inside pocket. "I appreciate it."

"That's OK," Clare smiled, "as long as you remember me when you're rich and famous."

Emma grinned. "Oh, come on..."

"You never know," the teacher said. "If that's what you want – go for it. Look at Alison Wyatt, David's sister. She made it. And if you won that you'd be well set.

24

You've got the ability," she dismissed Emma's protestations with a wave of her hand, "all you need now is a good story."

Emma glimpsed Jude through the railings, already heading into town. She shouted but Jude appeared not to hear. Emma walked on at her own pace. She had this competition thing to think about and did not feel like running.

Emma stood still as the idea dropped into her head. Of course. The Beresford case – twenty-five years on. It would be absolutely perfect.

Somewhere down the side road, a car started up. It approached the junction, where Emma was standing, fast and hardly slowed at all before pulling out into the oncoming traffic. Stupid idiot hadn't even looked. A horn blared and a van driver swore, waving two fingers out of his window.

Emma watched the car swerve into the school entrance and the driver get out. It was Wyatt. What was he doing skulking about down there when he should have been in school all morning?

Jude pushed herself back from the microfilm viewer and yawned, stretching her arms above her head to ease the tension in her back and shoulders. She'd got through loads of stuff. The Coombe Ashleigh murder had been big news at the time and there had been intense local interest in it.

"Found anything?"

She turned round. Emma was standing right behind her.

"Yeah. It's all here." She indicated the hopper between her knees that contained the copies she'd made of the relevant stories. "Not much on it now, though." She nodded towards the screen. "Being replaced by foot-and-mouth disease panic."

Emma leant forward to look over Jude's shoulder.

"When was this? 1968? Dig those miniskirts!" She scanned the page of the local paper and laughed. "Hey, they're still running that advert!"

"Is this just a social visit?" Jude asked as she brought up the next page. "Or are you disturbing me for some purpose?"

"I'm going back now." Emma said, shouldering her bag. "You coming?"

"No, I'm free for the rest of the afternoon so I'm going to stay and get on with this."

"Thought I'd come round tonight. Would about eight be OK?"

"Fine," Jude's gaze was back on the screen. "See you then."

"Ben's over there." Emma indicated the reference section where Ben Cooper was sitting with his books spread out. He didn't seem to be doing very much other than doodling with his pencil and staring at Jude.

"Yes," Jude replied without looking up, "I know. He's giving me a lift home."

"I see . . ."

"No you don't, Emma. It's just a lift, that's all. Now go away, I'm busy."

"OK, OK, I'm going. See you later."

*

Simon Freeman looked up as Emma walked past his enquiry desk.

"Thanks for your help," she said.

"That's OK. Any time," he said, with his best professional smile. "All part of the service."

He watched her go through the security gate and, as the doors swung back, he turned to his computer console and began tapping keys.

TASKER, EMMA
WHEELGATE FARM
BRIGHT LANE
COOMBE ASHLEIGH

He pulled over a pad, noted down the address and telephone number, and then scanned the rest of the information. A seventeen-year-old Scorpio; the DOB was still on her record from the children's section. Two fines unpaid and two books overdue. He checked the titles still out. What a person borrowed could often prove quite revealing.

He pressed ESCAPE and, as the screen went blank, he sat back, hands behind his head. He'd go up to the microfilm booth and see how her friend was getting on in a minute.

Jude turned the wheel and the borders of the page she was looking at disappeared. She turned it again. It was only a small item, a couple of lines towards the bottom of the page, but the names had attracted her attention:

MODERN YOUTH CONDEMNED

Local youths, Robert Arthur Wyatt, of Coombe

Ashleigh, and Gerald Allen Cooper of Hill Ashleigh, were both fined 25s and had a six months ban imposed on them by magistrates, following a string of motorcycling offences. Col. John Parker, chairman of the Bench, roundly condemned their actions, describing them as "symptomatic of the youth of today"

The rest was gone. A thick dark smudge right across it. Could "local youth, Gerald Allen Cooper" be Ben's dad? Must have been a bit of a tearaway when he was a lad. And how about Robert Arthur Wyatt? Was he any relation to Mr-totally-straight D. M. Wyatt BA MA, currently employed as head of History at the Sixth Form College? Amazing what you found out. Perhaps research could be fun, after all. Jude pressed the button on the front of the machine. The page blurred and disappeared as she obtained her photocopy.

"Need any help?"

Jude looked round, startled, to find the young library assistant standing behind her, hands in pockets.

"No, it's OK. I'm just finishing."

"How many photocopies have you done?" he said, nodding towards the hopper.

"Oh, I don't know." Jude reached down and handed them to him.

He sifted through them, counting them off. She had been thorough, he'd say that for her. She had found almost everything.

"Three pounds' worth so far," he said with a smile. "What's it for, a project?"

"Yeah," Jude said. "Local history. Case study."

"You ready, Jude?"

The dark boy from the reference section had come up and was standing by her table, arms folded.

"Yes," she said, "just got to pay for these."

Simon shrugged. "On the house."

"Thanks," she said, collecting them together.

"That's OK. Don't mention it."

"Hey, Ben. Look at this one. Is this your dad?"

Simon's pleasant have-a-nice-day smile faded as they clattered off down the stairs. Frowning, he rewound the film and put it back in the box marked 1967/1968. Had she found something? Something he had missed? It was possible. After all, she was obviously local. He had his own reasons to be interested in what had happened in Coombe Ashleigh twenty-five years ago, and had reviewed the papers for this year himself, more than once, in pursuit of those interests.

Chapter 5

"My, you have been busy," Emma said as she came through the door.

Her friend's bedroom resembled the incident room in a police station, with Jude sitting in the middle of the floor, at the centre of operations. All across one wall, the jumble of dolphin posters, art cards and likenesses of individuals Jude currently admired had been replaced by an interconnected display of maps, photocopied articles and groups of photographs.

In the centre, towards the top, was Jenny Beresford: a blurry black-and-white photo of a fat-faced little girl, long hair tied back in a bow, wearing a cardigan over a dress with smocking. To the right was a postcard of the Grange, the place where her mother had worked. It was now the Grange Hotel and Country Club, but then it had still been a private house and Jenny's mother had been the live-in cook-housekeeper. She had also been a single parent. Not long after the 22nd June, 1968, Emma read, the day she took little Jenny to the village fête, she had left the area. She had been committed to a hospital, somewhere near Birmingham, having suffered a severe breakdown. Jude did well to spot that, the article was so short it could have been a footnote.

"I brought this." Emma took a map from out of her pocket and spread it out. "Shows the village as it was then. I found it at home. There's the recreation ground where the fête was. And here're the allotments."

She indicated a point near the centre of the village. Jenny had been killed in one of the sheds. Jude pinned the map next to an article photocopied from the local paper. Emma checked the date. Two weeks after the event. Jude had underlined a police statement which read: "The discovery of certain evidence has led us to believe that we know the exact site where the crime was committed."

The whole area was new houses now. Emma wondered if any of the residents ever thought about it. They could be living right over the place where the little girl was murdered.

"Dead weird, don't you think?"

"What?" Emma glanced up. "Sorry, I wasn't listening."

"Those marks on her face. Look. Here. I suppose that's why they thought it was hippies."

Emma studied an artist's impression of Jenny Beresford. The drawing, pert and prettified, was made gruesome by the blankness of the eyes. Both cheeks were adorned with crude daisy-shaped flowers and the word "LOVE" was drawn in large capitals across the forehead.

"It didn't lead anywhere, though," Jude commented. "Says here no one could find anyone who could possibly have done it. The only ones living anywhere near had a cast-iron alibi. They'd been busted the day before for growing illegal substances."

"What about all the other people? The other ones who'd been at the fête?"

"Well, apparently, just like now, to get in, the Scouts stung you for a raffle ticket and you had to fill in your name and address. The police checked all the stubs. It

31

must have taken a long time but it was quite simple really. You know, it's funny," Jude frowned, "there were so many suspects at the beginning, the police didn't know where to start, and then one by one they were all eliminated and they ended up with nothing. It all came back to where it started – this village – and the case is still unsolved. A genuine mystery."

They were silent for a while. Jude sat down again and gathered her notes into a rough pile while Emma scrutinized each part of the display, studying the different things Jude had put up there more carefully.

"We've certainly got enough here to convince Clare," Emma said. "She gave me a lift home, I was talking to her about it on the way. She's still a bit iffy but I reckon she'll go for it. So – let's do it! List, list, list. What do we do first?"

"You've changed your tune," Jude said, regarding Emma with wary suspicion.

"I wouldn't say that . . ."

"Well, I would. Saturday, coming back on the bus, I got the distinct impression you wanted to pack in the whole project. What's happened to change your mind? Don't pretend, Emma. I know when you're up to something."

"I won't take it over if that's what you're worried about."

Jude shook her head. "That's not what I'm worried about. I sense some other private little Emma motive here and I want to know what it is or I'm not going on with it."

"OK, OK." Emma reached in her jacket and took out the competition details. "Here. Read this."

"Where did you get it?"

"Conrad. This morning. At first I couldn't think of anything – and then it suddenly came to me – "The Beresford Case". What do you think? You don't mind, do you? Me using what we find out as the basis for an article?"

Jude tried to read Emma's dark eyes as she folded the cutting and handed it back.

"No, of course I don't," she replied, stretching for a pad. "We'd better get on or you won't make the entry date."

Emma dropped down to the floor next to Jude and hugged her.

"You're the best friend . . ."

"Only friend," Jude corrected, without looking up. "No one else would put up with you. Now, have you had any other brilliant ideas, other than winning competitions and being famous?"

"Might have. One or two. The first thing to do is set up some interviews. Make a list of likely people. Get a pen."

Jude didn't move.

"I would have minded," she said after a moment, "I would have minded a lot, if you hadn't told me."

"But I did, didn't I? Here, use mine."

Emma produced a Parker biro from her inside pocket.

Jude frowned. "Don't hide things from me, Emma – and don't get too bossy." She picked up the pen. "Now then, who do you reckon would be good to talk to?"

"Well, it'll be no use going to just anyone. We need detail, things we can't find out from other sources . . ."

"What's the problem?" Jude caught Emma's thoughtful look. "Eileen Stanley is happy enough to talk about it."

"She's different." Emma hugged her knees. "People

round here have long memories, and not much happens so they won't have forgotten, but . . ."

"They won't talk about it?"

"Some won't. Others will talk but whether they'll tell you anything is a different matter. Even now they're pretty sensitive about it."

"Oh, come on!" Jude protested. "They can't still be sensitive about something that happened such a long time ago!"

"Why not? You said it yourself. When the leads dried up all the suspicion centred back on the village. That's why Russell came here to live."

"So who?" Jude drew a face on the blank pad. "I know! What about Clare Conrad and Mr Wyatt? They both lived here then. That reminds me. Does Wyatt have a brother?"

Emma shook her head.

"I don't know. Might, I suppose. He's got a sister, Alison . . ."

"I know, but we can hardly turn up at the BBC and ask to talk to her."

"Is it important? About the brother? I could ask Mum, she'd know."

"Not really. Just curiosity . . ." Jude went back to her list. "Do you think your mum would talk to us about the case?"

"Yes, I guess." Emma sat up. "I reckon a good way to start would be by asking Mum and Clare about it."

Marion, Emma's mother, and Clare Conrad were both from Coombe Ashleigh. Emma's mother baby-sat for Clare when she was little and when Emma was born, Clare reciprocated. They had become reacquainted since Clare's return to the area and were now close friends despite their age difference.

34

"But Emma, wait a minute," Jude said, "I've just thought of a fantastic drawback. When it happened," she calculated in her head, "they can't have been very old. They'd be small children!"

"My mum was eleven or twelve, that's hardly small," Emma said.

"OK – but Conrad can't have been more than five or six."

"So? I remember lots from when I was five or six."

"Yes, but it wasn't that long ago. I mean, we are talking more than twenty-five years here and she'd have been just a little kid."

"So was Jenny Beresford," Emma said as she stood up to go. "You just think about it."

Chapter 6

Clare Conrad was about four and three-quarters when Jenny Beresford was killed. That was about all she could say for certain when Jude and Emma finally caught up with her, leaving her classroom, on the following afternoon.

"I only remember that because I wasn't five until the end of September and I was worried they wouldn't let me go to school."

"But if you remember that," Emma persisted as they accompanied her down the corridor, "surely you can recall something about it. I mean, a murder is hardly an everyday event, is it?"

"Well, no. But memory is kind of . . . selective." The teacher turned to face them. "You remember what was important to you – especially at that age." She shifted the folders she was carrying on to her other hip and her clear grey eyes narrowed with thought. "It's difficult to sort out what's in my own memory from what I discovered later, or what other people told me a long time after." She turned her wrist to look at the oblong face of the thin gold man's watch she wore and her sharp-featured face tensed still further. "And, frankly, now's not a good time to ask me. I've got a meeting and I'm late already. I've got to go. Tell you what, I'll have a think about it and if I dredge up anything useful, you'll be the first to know."

"Great start," Emma observed as they watched her disappear through the staff-room door.

"Brilliant," Jude agreed ruefully. "Even for us. I hope it's not an omen . . ."

"Don't be daft," Emma said dismissively. "A minor setback, that's all."

"We could always try Wyatt," Jude suggested after a bit.

"Can't today," Emma replied. "He's not in school – again. Are you getting the bus home?"

"Well, er, no." Jude shook her head, hoping her hair would hide the fact that she was starting to blush. "Ben's giving me a lift home, actually."

"I see . . ." Emma's fine eyebrows rose and her dark eyes sparkled with speculation. "Do you think he'd give me one too?" she added in mock seriousness.

"Oh, yes. I guess so . . ."

Emma watched as reluctance and confusion heightened the colour on Jude's face, and laughed.

"Only kidding."

"Hey, Jude," Emma said as they looked across to where Ben was waiting in the car-park.

"Yes?"

"Take a tip from your Aunty Emma. Don't put up with any more of this on again, off again, lift home stuff. Get him to take you on a proper date!"

Clare Conrad got home late that evening. The meeting had gone on so long, she thought they were never going to get away. She stepped over the usual collection of junk mail and bills waiting for her on the mat, too tired even to bother to pick them up.

Bath first and then drink, she promised herself, after dropping her school bag just inside the door.

It had been a warm day, the sort that told you spring, summer even, was finally on its way. Clare unlocked the sliding glass door that led on to the balcony, feeling slightly more human after a bath and a change of clothes. It was getting dark now but it felt mild enough to sit out, for a while at least. She loved living here, loved the view it gave her. Even in the depths of winter, she'd wrap up well and then sit on the balcony for hours, sketching, writing, or just dreaming down at the river.

She put her feet on the rail and stared at the dark water. Somewhere a duck quacked and another called back, sounding like somebody laughing. Out in the central channel the white of a swan glimmered past and, on the opposite bank, blossom stood out bright as dusk gave way to night, and a faint breeze set the long, fine fronds of the weeping willows shifting and turning.

Some of her friends had thought her mad to come back, but it only took a minute or two out here to remember why she'd left London. Besides, she was only five minutes away from school instead of an hour or more if the traffic was bad; and although it was hard work sometimes, it was nothing compared to her previous job, in an inner city comprehensive, with its awesome web of stress inducing nightmare problems.

She was lost, watching the dark flowing water below, and her mind shifted on to a different track altogether. Ali. The thought came with a familiar twinge of guilt. They hadn't been in touch for a while, and although she liked living on her own, sometimes she really missed her. Clare looked at her watch. She might not be back yet. Perhaps later, she'd ring her.

Alison Wyatt. David's younger sister. Two people related by blood. Strange to utterly dislike one when you so liked the other.

Ali was the only thing about leaving London that she regretted at all. They had lived together, sharing a flat. It was Alison's really, Clare would never have been able to live in a place like that on a teacher's salary. They always got on well, respecting each other's space, rarely rowing or arguing. Ali was away a lot anyway, jetting out to the world's front lines and trouble spots. For weeks, Clare had the big apartment to herself and only saw her friend on the News. It was always a big kick to watch her, hear her say, "Alison Wyatt reporting."

Did she envy her? Sometimes. When Ali was somewhere exotic and Clare just faced another day in rainy London. But Clare admired her too much for such feelings to be anything more than fleeting.

Besides, they had been best friends for years. Grown up together. Although Ali was older, they had been in the same class in the tiny village school. When the time came for Clare to follow her to the Girls' Grammar, she had worried herself sick all that summer, thinking Ali would ignore her. She need not have been concerned. Ali always looked out for her. They caught the bus together and Ali never allowed the difference in their ages, so crucial to the other girls, to have the slightest effect on their relationship.

Like Emma and Jude, Clare thought, making the same journey every day from Coombe Ashleigh. She took a long drink and closed her eyes, letting her mind drift in time to the lapping of the river water.

*

39

"You aren't playing with us. Go away."

They were playing pooh-sticks. Jenny Beresford grabbed Clare's arm and twisted it sharply, making her drop the twig on the bridge instead of in the little stream. Hostile eyes, black and small like a teddy bear's, were very close, peering into Clare's as she tried to struggle away. Ali was already on the other side, watching with narrowed eyes to see whose came first. It was very bright. Midsummer light bounced and dazzled off the water.

"Why can't I?" Clare stood, small and defiant, looking over to Ali.

"Because it's my game and I said." Jenny's chubby face was close, flushed almost purple with the heat of the day and the outsize dressing-up clothes she was wearing. "And we don't want you, do we, Ali?"

Ali stood, lounging against the bridge, her striped T-shirt half in and half out of hand-me-down khaki shorts bunched at the waist with a snake belt. The fancy dress competition was over now and she had removed the checked handkerchief pirate's scarf. Her bright red hair fell over her freckled forehead into her pale blue eyes. Remnants of a beard and moustache shadowed her face and the string of a makeshift eye-patch dangled from her pocket. Clare looked to her for judgement, small features creased with a mixture of pleading and hero worship.

Ali shrugged and stuck her thumbs in her stripy belt.

"It's her game, Clare. Go back to the fête. Come on, Jenny."

Jenny Beresford twisted the beads she wore and sent them swinging back and forth, smirking in triumph. She grabbed Ali's arm and went clacking off, strutting in her mother's high heels, down the lane that led to the allotments.

Clare had followed them at a distance, determined to spy. But when she got to the allotments they were nowhere to be seen. She had stood alone among the dishevelled rows of vegetables, howling her eyes out. She remembered the smell choking in the back of her throat. Sweet williams. Jewelled colours on dark green brittle stems, some lay wilting on the path, scattered about, others stretched away from her in a thick stand that seemed almost as tall as she was, breathing out a scent of overpowering sweetness.

The sound of the telephone jarred Clare back to consciousness and she almost spilt her drink. When she went to get up, her right knee was locked and her foot had gone to sleep. She eased her legs off the balcony rail and hobbled indoors, picking up the receiver just as it was switching over to the answerphone.

"Hello, it's me. Ignore all that," she said, overriding her own voice.

"Hello, you." The voice was unmistakable, low and musical, tinged with amusement. Clare felt the pleasure at hearing it spreading through her.

"Hello, Ali. I was just thinking about you." She cradled the phone to her and lay down on the sofa. "Synchronicity."

Ali laughed. "Still working for us, then?"

Clare smiled. "Seems to be. Hang on a minute. I've got to shut the balcony."

"What's it like there?" Ali asked when she came back.

"Nice. Spring-like. It was today, anyway."

"It's pissing with rain here."

Clare pictured Ali staring at the lights of London,

spreading out and away from her, refracted through the raindrops on her window.

"Well," she laughed, "that's got the weather out of the way. How's it going?"

"Oh, you know. Usual parade of scumbags, slime balls, low-life types and con men."

Clare smiled. Ali didn't go abroad any more. She had her own programme now. Fearless and persistent, she went about exposing scams, cons and injustices, jamming her foot in the door of the corrupt and inefficient, championing ordinary people. Strong men visibly paled on screen, and more than a few had made a run for it when they'd seen the camera and heard her say, "My name is Alison Wyatt and I'm here to ask you a few questions . . ."

"Look, Clare . . ." Her voice had changed, the tone dismissing further small talk. "I need to . . . can I come and see you? Maybe stay for a day or two?"

"Yes, of course." Clare thought about asking why and then thought again. "When?"

"Next week sometime. It's been crazy here but it's slackening off. I've got some stuff to finish, then they owe me a few days' holiday."

"Great. Whenever. I'll look forward to it."

"Good. That's really good, Clare." The relief in her voice was both palpable and puzzling. "I'll let you know exactly when I'm coming. And, Clare . . ."

"Yes?"

"Don't tell anyone, will you?"

By anyone she meant her brother, David.

"No, of course not. Not if you don't want me to."

"OK. Right. That's fine. See you soon then?"

"Yes, see you."

But Ali had already rung off. Clare went to the hall to

get her bag. She'd put it off long enough. Those essays weren't marking themselves in there and she'd promised to return them to their anxious owners in her Upper Sixth group first thing tomorrow morning.

Before she settled down to it, she started to write out what she'd remembered about Jenny Beresford to give to Jude and Emma. In mid-sentence she stopped and stared down at her writing. She and Ali had probably been the last people to see Jenny Beresford alive, except for whoever killed her. Had they been asked about it? They must have been, surely? Maybe Ali would know. Clare had no recollection of ever having told a living soul what she was writing now. She hadn't even known she knew about it herself until an hour or so ago.

Chapter 7

David Wyatt was the next person on Jude's interview list, but she wasn't sure if it was good news or bad news when she found out that he was in school and wanted to see her at eleven o'clock that morning.

"Come."

The command came at her second knock. She entered the room. He looked up to see long denim-clad legs walking towards him. His eyes focused on the intricately worked silver buckle of a wide leather belt that cinched her waist in tightly. His gaze travelled up her body and rested on her face.

"I'm Judith Hughes," she said. "You wanted to see me."

She was attractive. Very attractive. With that long golden hair spilling down over her shoulders. Some of them shouldn't be allowed. Dealing with that every day – you ought to be paid danger money! He coughed slightly and looked away, trying to dismiss what he was thinking. Sometimes it was as though his brother took over his mind. Robbie's thoughts suddenly appeared like grit in his own head, as coarse as sea salt.

Her white shirt tightened as she breathed in and out. She was nervous. He looked at her face; clear, even features and near flawless skin. Pretty. Very pretty. Her dark blue eyes were clouded in doubt but her full mouth was tentatively smiling.

Jude crossed her arms defensively and her jaw tightened. He noticed a rather pronounced cleft in her chin as she looked down at him and repeated what she had said previously.

"You wanted to see me."

"Yes. About this."

He sifted the submission on his desk. She had to lean over to see what he was pointing at. He caught a breath of some clear, sweet perfume as she leant in towards him.

"Where did you get these?"

The beads round Jude's neck had swung out in front of him and he was holding on to them. Jude was caught, awkwardly bent over his desk; if she pulled away they'd break. She was held close for a second, staring into china-blue eyes, the sandy lashes and fine lines magnified by his glasses. Then he let go. She stood up and the beads swung back out of his reach. She caught them to her and held them.

"I – I made it myself," she said, looking down at the necklace. She separated the beads out, telling them like a rosary. "I got these green glass ones in a junk shop. The silver ones and the others I had already."

"They are very . . ." he searched for the right word, "unusual. You have quite a talent. Do you make things to sell? My wife likes unusual jewellery."

"Well, er," Jude didn't quite know what to say, "not usually. I generally make things for myself or for friends, you know," she shrugged, "Christmas or birthdays."

"It's my wife's birthday – this weekend." He paused and swung round in his chair. "You wouldn't sell me those, would you? I'd give you a good price. I've been looking for something different."

45

"Oh, hey, I don't know . . ." Jude felt embarrassed, at a loss for what to say.

"It was just an idea," he said, dismissing it with a wave of his hand. "Think about it."

"Yeah, OK. Meanwhile . . ."

He was staring at his blank computer screen now as though she wasn't there.

"Meanwhile what?"

"What about my submission for the local history project?"

"I think the subject choice ill-advised. Are you doing it on your own?"

"No. I'm doing it with Emma Tasker."

"Her name doesn't appear here."

"That's because I wrote that. But Emma is doing it too. Ms Conrad knows about it."

His hand trembled slightly as he gathered up the proposal and handed it back to her. He had to force himself not to stare at the beads. Laughter bubbled like vomit in his throat. This was too much, even for a sense of irony as black and bitter as his. Of all the topics they could have chosen, why this? If only he'd been in school he could have put a stop to that at least. Instinct told him it was too late now. To intervene would just draw attention, especially with Emma Tasker involved. She'd start wanting to know why. He couldn't risk that. Better to let them carry on with it.

"Well, as I say, I'm not entirely happy with your chosen topic, but since Ms Conrad has approved it and you've already started . . .'

"Thanks, Mr Wyatt."

Jude collected her work and was already backing out. She closed the door and leant against the wall.

Boy, was he weird! She did not envy Emma one little bit. She was glad she didn't have him as a teacher.

Chapter 8

"What do you mean you didn't ask him?"

"What I said. I didn't ask him."

"Why not?"

"I don't know . . ."

It was another warm day. They had gone down to the river at lunch-time to eat their sandwiches and feed the ducks.

Jude sighed. She could not explain exactly why but the whole interview had made her feel really uncomfortable, scared even, and she'd just wanted to get out of there as quickly as possible.

"Well," she said in the end, "there just didn't seem to be an opportunity."

"God, Jude." Emma lobbed a crust viciously at an approaching drake, nearly hitting him on the head. 'I'll have to ask him then, won't I? We've got him this afternoon." She snorted with disgust and tore up another crust. "Sometimes you are just so wimpy."

"Excuse me, Mr Wyatt, may I ask you something?"

Gathering his notes at the end of the lesson, he glanced up to see Emma Tasker approaching his desk with her confident, gliding, ballet dancer's walk. She was too tall and thin for his taste and he had never liked her. Right from the first lesson, although he could never catch her at it, he'd had this feeling she was somehow laughing at him. Her almost excessive politeness amounted to insolence in his book and he endured her dark-eyed, appraising stare with more and more difficulty. What this girl was thinking, what was going on behind that face, you couldn't even begin to guess. Now, as she perched herself on the side of his desk and made her request, he found himself clutching his texts, frilled with thin curling reference markers, and his battered old files, more tightly to his chest.

"What exactly is your involvement in this, Emma? I was led to understand that this was Judith Hughes's topic."

Emma shrugged, swinging her legs before pushing herself off the desk.

"I don't know who or what let you to understand that, sir. We are doing it together."

"Well, you'll have to ask somebody else," he said as he headed for the door. "I'm certainly not helping you with such a dubious project."

"That's what he called it," Emma said to Jude as they went to catch the bus. "A dubious project."

"Charming."

"I don't think we'll get very much out of him."

"What about his brother?"

"What brother?"

"The one I saw about in the paper. You were going to ask your mother."

"Sorry, Jude. I totally forgot. I'll ask her later."

"Quick! The bus!"

The rest of the conversation was lost in the scramble

to get on. Emma pushed up towards the back and found a place where they could sit together.

"No lift tonight, eh? Slumming it with the rest of us. All these people and all this crush." Emma shook her head in mock sympathy. "How are you going to stand it, Jude?"

"He's got football practice," Jude replied. "But I saw him between lessons this afternoon and he gave me this."

She delved in her bag and fished out a thick cream-coloured envelope.

"Nice paper," Emma commented as she peered inside. "It isn't what I think it is?"

"What might that be?"

"An invitation to Caroline Grainger's eighteenth birth-day party."

"You needn't look like that." Jude produced an ident-ical envelope from the front pocket of her rucksack. "Ben asked her for two. This one's for you."

Chapter 9

David Wyatt started his car as the school bus pulled away. Why was he following them? It was ridiculous. They were just a couple of schoolgirls. On the bus. Off the bus. Regular as clockwork. He knew where they came from and where they went. Where else would they be going?

I'm just paying a visit to Mum's, he said to himself, to check on things.

He slotted his white Escort in behind the yellow-and-black bus, keeping a couple of vehicles back, all the way to the village. A turn of the head was enough to see the two girls get off and he drove past.

Halfway up the steep hill, David slowed and changed gear to take the hidden bend. He negotiated the narrowing, pot-holed road leading on to Mitre Hill with care and the trees closed in around him.

The car pulled up in front of two cottages, built together and standing slightly off the road. Not particularly picturesque, nineteenth-century functional red brick, they looked like the kind of dwellings found in rows and rows near the centre of any small town, except these stood on their own, huddling against each other for protection, dwarfed by big trees. Dark, deserted and lifeless, their straggling gardens were surrounded by overgrown hedges fast returning to forest. Estate agents' signs indicated that both properties were for sale. One board was new. The other, warped and weathered, tilted over sideways, half falling down.

David stood for a moment, welcomed by the silence of the woods. Then a bird flew past his head, hammering out a sudden alarm call, making him jump. He hurried to the peeling porch built on the side of the right-hand cottage and let himself in.

As he entered, he fought down an automatic desire to shout out, "Mum, I'm home!" He prowled around. Just being here was enough to relax him, even though it was dark and cold, and his heels rang on bare boards through rooms empty of furniture.

He slid down the wall and sat in the corner of what had been his room – and Robbie's. He took a bottle from his pocket and unscrewed the cap. The floor was dusty, wind whined through warped sills and damp crept down from the eaves, but he liked it better than the centrally-heated comfort of the house he lived in now.

He closed his eyes, picturing how the room had been. It wasn't difficult. His mother had kept this room exactly how it was when he and Robbie had lived at home, until the day she died.

He'd wanted to move back, but Elizabeth had not wanted that. The house was too small, she said, too damp, too isolated. She had turned to with a will, though, to help him sort out the contents, putting on her rubber gloves, classifying, cataloguing, selecting and rejecting in her usual capable way.

Ali didn't want anything.

"I don't have room," she had said at the funeral, "and besides . . ." She had shrugged and crossed her arms, leaving the rest of the sentence to dangle.

And Robbie was no longer around, so what they

couldn't keep themselves, Elizabeth had negotiated for Jed Cooper to come and haul away.

He took a drink and swung the bottle between his knees, his mind slipping back. He should not have left it all up to her. He should have taken more of an interest.

But all he had done during that terrible week was wander around the house. Stunned and dazed by grief, he'd just watched as his mother's things got piled and boxed, like the results of an archaeological dig, each item tagged and labelled with memories. He'd begun sifting through, looking for what to keep, but soon he'd felt overwhelmed by the sheer mass and Elizabeth had taken over with her cool efficiency.

That is when she must have found them. Maybe she'd opened a drawer at random, heard something rattle at the back, reached in and there they were, perhaps in one of Dad's old tobacco tins or in a matchbox. The beads. His heart seemed to slow in his chest and then speed up at the thought of it. Elizabeth hadn't known what they were, what they meant. How could she? He might curse himself for a fool now, but even he had almost forgotten they'd ever existed. She would have discarded them after one glance, as too insignificant to even consult him about.

He remembered them now. Glimmering green. He even recalled the feel of them, his memory reading like braille the intricate patterning. She was a strange one, his mother. He thought she had got rid of them, and all these years they had been right here. Why had she kept them? He'd never know now. He could never ask her. He could never again ask her anything.

He remembered them, dropping on to the scratched and scarred top of the bureau. Nine beads. He'd counted them out, dropping back into the ways of childhood.

One for Ali. One for me. One for Robbie.

"What are we going to do now?"

"What goes around, comes around, brother."

Robbie had reached down and gathered them up as a gambler might a set of dice. He had blown into his palm then, and shaken them, and when he opened his fist, David had seen an empty hand. The beads had vanished.

"Gone now," Robbie had said. "Like pebbles cast on a beach of pebbles. Safe exit."

Robbie had dropped them out of his sight, out of his consciousness. Now they had resurfaced. Found in a junk shop, among the bric-à-brac and bits and pieces, fetched up on the reef of small objects people acquire through their lives. So many things collected only to be discarded.

Found by a girl who turns up wearing them, right there in his office. Chance? Maybe. Right this minute it felt more like fate than coincidence.

"What are we supposed to do about that?" he shouted aloud. "Hey, Robbie?"

Don't over-react, the voice came back. Just keep an eye on the situation. Easy to say, harder to do, especially when he felt like this all the time, ready to explode, ready to shatter at a single touch.

"I'm right on the edge," he muttered, passing a hand over his sweating face. "I don't know how much more I can take. I'm right on the edge of something."

He took another swallow from the bottle and then hurled it away. The glass smashed, high on the wall. The contents spread out in a starburst stain and the room filled with whisky fumes, sweetish, overpowering.

Chapter 10

"Have you got the extra batteries?"

Jude nodded and patted her pocket.

"And the spare tape?"

"Yes, a new C90." Jude showed Emma. "Surely that's enough? Even Mrs Stanley can't talk that much."

"Want to bet?" Emma said with a tilt of her head.

"Well, let's hope she does. You never know, she might tell us something we can use."

"Depends what kind of mood she's in. She's still our best bet, though, at the moment."

Only bet, Jude thought. They'd talked to plenty of people over the past few days but, so far, no one had told them anything remotely useful. OK, it was a long time ago, but surely it was the kind of day that stuck in the memory, like the Kennedy assassination? But no. People either couldn't remember, or muttered that it was best forgotten. Even those who did dredge up something to say only mentioned things they already knew. It was frustrating.

Mrs Stanley's house was one of eight, on a recently built estate, in a pocket of development near the centre of the village. Jude peered through the leaded double glazing. It was odd, she commented as Emma rang the ding-dong bell, why get a new house cross-hatched with mock beams and fake leading, when the real thing was practically next door? The Stanleys weren't short of a bob or two. Reg Stanley owned the local garage and his wife was no Mrs Overall, she had her own company. "No job too small for We-Do-It-All" said the ads she ran in the local paper.

"She's as deceptive as her house," Emma warned before they went in. "Don't underestimate her."

"Hello, it's open," a voice shouted. "Come on through. I've been expecting you."

Mrs Stanley was waiting for them in her spacious modern kitchen. A big pot of tea was already on the table, flanked by a plate of Mr Kipling cakes and various brands of chocolate biscuit.

"How do you take your tea, girls?"

"Oh, uh, as it comes," Emma said for both of them. "No sugar."

Mrs Stanley poured the brew into two brightly coloured mugs.

"I hope you like it strong. I can't abide these weak fancy blends some of my ladies get from Sainsbury's. I take my own Typhoo."

Most of Mrs Stanley's "ladies" were newcomers who had moved to the area in recent years. Their large houses demanded considerable upkeep and most of the occupants had neither the time nor the inclination to do the housework themselves. So Eileen Stanley did it for them. She employed her own daughters and several village girls now and had built up a solid business.

"What an Ooh can do, eh?" she grinned and winked as she planted the steaming mugs in front of them.

She lit a cigarette and regarded them with narrowed eyes through a plume of smoke.

"Now, how can I help you two?"

She was a big woman but solidly built rather than fat. Her flesh gave her presence and smoothed her face, preserving and making handsome what must have been, in her youth, a rather bland prettiness. Her mid-length fair hair was subtly highlighted to hide any grey and softly permed. Emma said she was about forty-five but Jude would have found it impossible to tell by looking at her how old she was.

She belonged, like Emma, to one of the old families. The churchyard contained rows of Stanley graves. She knew everything about what had happened in the past, what was happening now, and what was likely to happen in this village, and that kind of knowledge equals power in such a small community.

"We . . ." Jude started.

"We just want to ask you a few questions, Mrs S," Emma took over, "and we'd like to use this," she indicated the tape recorder, "if you don't mind?"

Mrs Stanley looked slightly nonplussed at the sight of the tape recorder but nevertheless nodded her assent.

"No, I don't mind. Ask away," she said.

"Interview. Mrs Eileen Stanley. Eighteenth of March," Emma said as she depressed the RECORD button. "Emma Tasker and Jude Hughes, researching the Beresford case. Now, Mrs Stanley, perhaps you wouldn't mind . . ."

Jude noted what the tape machine could not, the veiled look that came into the blue eyes and quickly passed across the older woman's deceptively open face. They were going to get blanked out again if they were not very careful.

"Could I have a biscuit?" she asked suddenly. "Clubs are my favourite."

"And mine. Take one. Take two. I bought them for

57

you." Mrs Stanley stubbed out her cigarette and took a biscuit herself, unwrapping it deftly. "I'm supposed to be on a diet, but one won't hurt."

She demolished it in two bites and began unwrapping another.

"Emma's mum said you work as a home help, you know, helping the elderly."

"Yes, that's right, love. Social don't pay much but I wouldn't let it go. I've been with some of them for years and old folk don't like change. And, besides, you don't know what types are doing it nowadays."

"My Nan and Gramps have a home help," Jude said, ignoring Emma's questioning look. "Her name's Sarah. They didn't want anyone at first but now they don't know what they'd do without her."

"That's what I mean." Mrs Stanley's heavy charm bracelet tinkled and shook as she dusted crumbs from her raspberry angora sweater with a plump, ringed hand. "They get very dependent and you get fond of them. It's a terrible wrench when one of them goes."

"Goes?" Jude looked puzzled, then she understood. "Dies, you mean?"

"Yes. Want more tea? Just top you up. You, dear?" Emma shook her head. "It doesn't happen all that often, touch wood, but when it does it certainly shakes you up. It's almost like one of your own going. I mean, take poor old Jack Russell . . ."

Jude glanced down to see that the tape was going round and gently nudged Emma's leg under the table.

"I just popped my head round to tell him his spot of dinner was all ready in the microwave and I knew straight away he'd gone. He was all crumpled over, caught up on one side like, just where he sat. Went the same way as my old mum. And I never heard a thing – upstairs hoovering. Can be a blessing in some ways – saves 'em lingering on in pain, but . . ."

"Did he have something else wrong with him, then?" Jude asked.

"Yes," Mrs Stanley nodded solemnly. "Cancer."

"Oh," Jude said, surprised, "I didn't know that."

"Oh, yes." Mrs Stanley poured herself more tea. "I saw the results of the tests he'd had when I was tidying up . . .'

I bet you did, Emma thought, probably knew more than the doctors.

"Did he ever talk to you about the Beresford case?" Emma cut in.

Eileen Stanley cocked her head on one side and her blue eyes sharpened.

"No, he didn't.'

"Never?"

"Not recent. He seemed to have gone inside himself about it. But it was still eating away at him. Could be that caused the cancer. It can do, you know . . ."

"Did, uh, did it cause resentment when he first came here? Him being who he was?" Jude said, trying a different tack. "Did it cause a lot of resentment in the village?"

"Yes, of course it did." Eileen Stanley sounded impatient. Emma looked up, dark eyes alert. That question had struck home. "He said to all the newspapers that someone from Coombe Ashleigh murdered that child. Even him coming to live here was a story on its own. 'Sinister Village of Shame,' the *News of the World* called us. How would you feel? Of course it was resented. Some were all for freezing him out, but I said let it be. And I was right. All those years and he never found nothing, did he? Besides, he was nice was old Jack, a pleasure to work for, not like some of them – always moaning on about . . ."

"Who do you think did it, then?" Emma asked suddenly.

Jude opened her mouth to say something but Emma motioned her to be quiet and leant forward, elbows on the table. She was fast losing patience with this. Eileen Stanley was playing with them. She could chatter on all day, letting slip bits here and there but not really telling them anything. It was time to come clean and ask straight out what they wanted to know. Odds were she'd show them the door, but Emma had observed her for years. She was a strange woman, not at all what she seemed, and there was an outside chance she'd answer.

"Come on, Eileen. You know everything that happens round here. Who killed little Jenny? You must have some idea."

Eileen Stanley stared at her for a moment, considering, and then reached for her cigarettes.

"You want one?" She offered the packet. "Please yourself but I know you smoke. How about you?" Jude shook her head in refusal. "Turn that thing off," she indicated the tape recorder, "and I'll tell you what I think."

She lit her cigarette, cupping her hands round the lighter, and then sat back, ready to start her story.

"I reckon they're dead and gone. They can't be got for it now. So what's the harm in talking to you two about it?" She paused, squinting at them through a stream of smoke. "It wasn't a great village conspiracy, everyone covering up for everyone else like Jack Russell thought." She laughed, wheezing and mirthless, and picked a bit of filter off her tongue. "Never let it alone, Jack wouldn't, like a dog with a bone. Perhaps he'll be satisfied, now he's gone and joined them." She tapped her ash and watched them shrewdly. "Like I said, it wasn't no conspiracy. It was more a case of no one telling the truth and the whole truth about what they were up to on the day little Jenny went missing."

"How do you mean, Mrs Stanley?" Jude asked. "They all say they don't remember."

"Is that so?" Eileen Stanley's eyebrows quirked up in disbelief. "They remember all right, they was asked about it often enough and they all had their stories."

"You mean they were all lying?"

"Not all. Most didn't have anything to hide. Those that did . . . Well, I wouldn't say it was lying exactly . . ."

Suddenly she was looking straight at Jude.

"I mean, do you?" she asked. "Do you tell everyone the truth all the time? Like what you were doing parked off the road in young Ben Cooper's car the other afternoon?"

Jude glanced away.

"I – we – " she looked about helplessly, starting to blush, "we were just talking!"

"Oh, just talking," Eileen Stanley said, with mock solemnity. "That's what they call it nowadays, is it? And you can stop laughing, Emma Tasker. Things I know about what you were getting up to with that Joe Thompson last summer'd turn you the colour of our hall carpet. No," she said, contemplating the glowing end of her cigarette, "truth is tricky stuff. Slippery."

Just like you, Emma thought, as she surreptitiously depressed the RECORD button.

"There were a few not telling the truth about that afternoon. I know I wasn't." She laughed softly to herself. "And there were just as many covering up. That's the way things were. All the coppers in the world couldn't make us say any different. Tea's gone cold. I'll pop the kettle back on. Anyone fancy another?"

"What were you doing then?" Emma asked.

"I was in town. Meeting my friend Janet for a bit of Saturday shopping, just like you do now. Sid Cootes, the conductor – buses had conductors in them days – remembered me going in on the bus . . ."

Eileen Stanley came back to the table with a fresh pot of tea.

"Funny little kid she was, Jenny I mean. Sure you don't want a cup?" The two girls shook their heads. "Lived up at the Hall with her mother. Anna Beresford was cook-housekeeper to the Harrisons. He was a solicitor, retired, from Bristol way – pots of money. Anyway, Mrs Harrison took a real shine to Jenny – no kids of her own, see? Always giving her things for dressing up – silk shawls, beads – all kinds of stuff, some of it quite expensive."

"So – so what were you really doing?" Emma asked, impatiently. "If you said you were in town, but you were not telling the truth, where were you?"

"Just like your dad, aren't you?" Mrs Stanley gave Emma an appraising look. "Straight to the point, no messing. Well, I'll tell you. I did go to town but Janet didn't turn up, so I came back early. Fête was on but I wasn't going anywhere near that. Mum was doing teas and, if she'd seen me, she'd have had a pinny round me in a flash. No, I was on my way home when I met someone."

"Who?"

"A chap I knew, does it matter? Anyway – we got back home. No one in, house to ourselves. All at the fête, see? We were upstairs – doing a bit of courting . . ."

She caught the look of astonishment that passed between Emma and Jude and burst into ribald laughter.

"Oh, Miss Prim and Miss Proper! I didn't always look like this, you know. That's the trouble with people your age – think you invented it, don't you!" She sat back and wiped her eyes on a tea towel. "I suppose we did too. Swinging Sixties, the Pill and all that, but my mum'd have killed me if she'd found out. Anyway, like I said we was upstairs, getting dressed by then, when suddenly there was a real commotion, shouting out the back, hammering on the Wyatt's door. I went to the window to see what's going on, and there's David Wyatt going hysterical, in a terrible state he was, and their Robbie's trying to calm him down. Then old Ma Wyatt comes out, wiping her hands on her pinafore. They're talking real close and fierce. I was trying to hear and I must have moved the curtain or something because, all of a sudden, she's looking straight at me. Then her eyes kind of flick behind, and I know she's seen the lad I was with. She had these dark little curranty eyes, set deep in her head, and her mouth was a tight little gash. If the floor could have swallowed me up . . ." she shivered slightly at the memory. "Old Ma Wyatt wasn't one to cross."

Emma was sitting listening, one elbow on the table, hand supporting her chin. She moved her head slightly to show that she understood. Jude frowned. Somehow she'd missed something.

"I'm sorry," she said, shaking her head. "I don't understand."

Mrs Stanley's eyes narrowed on her and then she looked away.

'I've told you enough, more than enough. Old Ma

Wyatt was off the hill. Not to be crossed." She looked hard at Emma. "You know what I mean. You tell her."

"Yes. Yes, I will." Emma nodded and stood up. "Thank you very much for seeing us, Eileen. You've been very helpful."

Jude followed Emma out. She didn't exactly understand this last exchange, but one thing was crystal clear, the interview with Eileen Stanley was well and truly over.

Chapter 11

"What did she mean?" Jude said as soon as they were outside.

Emma put a gloved finger to her lips.

"Not here. We'll go back to your house."

Emma didn't speak again until they were upstairs in Jude's bedroom. She plugged the tape recorder in next to the bed and pressed REWIND. She stopped and pressed PLAY. Jude heard herself say, "I'm sorry, I don't understand . . ." Emma flicked it off and threw herself on to the bed.

"Oh, thank God," she said, "it's recorded."

"OK, so what did she mean? What was all that stuff about Mrs Wyatt being off the hill and not someone to mess with?"

Emma rolled over and looked up at Jude. Her shiny hair fell forward and the expression in her dark, greeny-brown eyes was difficult to read.

"You won't like it."

"How do you know?"

Emma rolled back and lay with her hands behind her head, staring up at the ceiling.

"She was talking about witchcraft."

Jude's eyes widened in horror.

"Witchcraft! You've got to be joking!"

"You did ask." Emma sighed and closed her eyes. "I knew you wouldn't like it."

"I thought it was all a figment of the press – all this witchcraft business."

"Well, it is and it isn't. I mean, it's based on fact.' Emma's eyes opened wide again. "This whole area is steeped in stories about witches and ghosts and things like that. People seeing lights in the middle of the night, up on the hill. They say covens used the hill for their meetings." Emma sat up. "Mitre Hill wasn't always called that, you know."

"I thought it was called that because of its shape."

"No," Emma shook her head, "it was blessed and sanctified by some bishop and christened that to make it more holy and banish evil things. But there have always been rumours about strange happenings up there and the people off the hill have always had a certain reputation."

"You aren't one, are you?"

"What?"

"A witch?"

Jude was not entirely joking and Emma's reply was quite serious when she said,

"No. It's not in my family."

"You don't believe in it, surely? Charms and covens and that?"

"No, I don't. But there's some round here that do, my dear," she said parodying Mrs Stanley's slight rural accent. "Really. I think they only used charms when people did believe in them. Nowadays they operate in a different way."

"How do you mean, 'they'?"

Jude looked at her, puzzled. Despite what she'd just said, Emma was using the present tense.

"Well, OK. Listen. In the old days there were women – and men – who knew things the others didn't and could

do things they couldn't and they used this knowledge –
often for good – but sometimes for evil. It gave them
power and people were frightened of them." Emma sat
up, shaking her head to deny Jude's protestations.
"Honestly. There are documented cases of murder based
on witchcraft in this area, in this century. I think these
people are still here, but they work it differently."

"For example?"

"Eileen Stanley."

"Mrs Stanley!" Jude said incredulously. "You can't
have a witch wearing pink angora and blue eyeliner!
Anyway, she's too heavy – she'd break the broomstick!"

"No, I don't mean like that! I don't mean she belongs
to covens and that sort of thing. What I mean is, Mrs
Stanley knows a lot about people. She knows their secrets.
That makes her powerful. Not someone to cross, like she
said about old Mrs Wyatt. Only now, she's it."

"How do you mean? I don't follow."

"OK," Emma's slim expressive hands spread out,
describing a space in front of her. "Mrs S and her girls
'do' a lot of the houses for miles around. She helps my
mum two mornings a week, I bet she's even helped yours
on occasions."

Jude nodded. "Last year spring-cleaning and in the
summer, helping Mum make curtains."

"Right. Now you can be absolutely sure, every house
she goes in, she comes out knowing all about the people
who live there, from what sort of breakfast cereal they
eat, and toothpaste they prefer, to what sort of sex
they have and how often they have it. Plus, the current
state of their bank balance and how much they've paid
off on their Barclaycard."

"So what?"

"So a lot of it is probably useless information but even so, it's not things you want everyone to know, is it? And once in a while I bet she comes across some real little nuggets. I keep my door locked. I'm serious! I won't let her go in there. And she's always going on about it. She doesn't like it at all."

"What does she do with this information? Blackmail people?"

Emma laughed. "Nothing so crude! She just lets you know she knows, that's all. Like you and Ben – you didn't even tell *me* about that – and me and Joe Thompson last summer."

"You didn't tell *me* about that!"

"It was ages ago. I didn't know you that well then."

"Who is he, anyway?"

"A reporter on the *Gazette*."

Jude wanted to ask more but knew from Emma's face that it was a closed subject.

"And I didn't know you smoked," she said instead.

Emma shrugged. "I don't. Now. It was a mistake. So was Joe. They kind of went together."

"OK." Jude sighed. "But I still don't see how stuff like that can possibly be of any use to anyone, let alone Mrs Stanley."

"It's not what you know, it's what you do with it that counts. She drops bits and snippets into conversations. It stirs up distrust. What do you think she was doing with us? And it gets you wondering how much more she knows, and who she's going to tell about it. Don't you see? It gives her power. She uses it like a weapon as well, to hurt people."

"Like how? Give me an example."

68

Emma thought for a moment, then she said, "All right. But you won't like this, either."

"Tell me!"

"Ever since she's known about you and Ben, she's been making little remarks about him and Caroline Grainger. Like yesterday she was telling me apropos of absolutely nothing, how every time she dusts his photograph, which is, of course, next to Caroline's bed, she can't help thinking how they made a lovely couple."

Jude did not reply. Ben and Caroline had split with each other at the beginning of the year. It had not occurred to her that it might not be over.

"Of course she's telling me because she knows I'm your friend," Emma added, "and I'll report back to you about it."

"Thanks, Emma. I could work that out for myself," Jude replied frostily. "I'm not entirely stupid. Sorry, I didn't mean to snap." She shook her head. "And I thought Mrs Stanley was just the village gossip."

"That's just her act. She's very far from that. Believe me, she's dangerous."

Jude went to the wall and looked at the various stages of their Beresford case research.

"We still aren't much further on with this, though," she said, tracing the various pages with her fingers. "She didn't tell us more than anyone else has, really."

Emma came over and stood beside her.

"Oh, yes she did. She told us about the Wyatts, for one thing." She took a pin and stuck it in the side of Mitre Hill. "She put them on the map, that's for certain."

Jude touched the smudged grainy image of Jenny Beresford.

"Do you think she knows who did it?"

69

"She knows all right. Or thinks she does."

"So why didn't she inform the police?"

Emma rolled her eyes. "Haven't you been listening to anything? She wouldn't waste information like that on a bunch of coppers. Besides, she might have had her own reasons for keeping it to herself."

Emma picked up the tape from the bedside table.

"I'm going to take this home and transcribe it, see if it contains any more coded messages. The question is," she added as she put the cassette in her pocket and pulled on her gloves, "why keep it secret all these years and then tell us about it? See you, Jude."

"Yes," Jude replied, "see you tomorrow."

Jude returned slowly to her room. Witchcraft. She couldn't handle that. This whole thing was beginning to give her the creeps. She stared at the wall with all the pictures. On the map of the village, the little blocks of buildings seemed to merge and coalesce into broken teeth. Contours and spidery pathways spread like wrinkled lines, the dark patches of woodland on Mitre Hill provided deep eye-sockets and hollow cheeks, until she began to see the sinister sketch of a lopsided face leering out at her.

Jenny Beresford's features were real enough. What would she have looked like now? Jude wondered. She would be about Clare Conrad's age if she'd lived. Probably have a career, marriage, kids.

Suddenly, marking areas out, where she'd been killed, where she'd been found, with bright stars and thin, red ribbon, seemed cheap and lurid. As she scanned the wall, all the other stuff, grey dead photographs and forensic details, seemed to crowd in on her as well, leaving her feeling slightly nauseated.

She began taking it all off. Working slowly at first and then tearing at it, not caring if corners got ripped or the wallpaper came away in strips. Tomorrow she'd go and tell Clare. It had all been a hideous mistake. She would ask to start a new project.

Chapter 12

"What do you mean you haven't got it?" Emma was standing in the middle of the road refusing to budge.

"I – I don't want to do it any more. I'm going to see Conrad this morning. I want to change assignment. Come on, we'll miss the bus."

Jude took her arm but Emma pulled away.

"Oh, no. Not when we're finally getting somewhere." She shook her head. "I spent half the night transcribing that bloody tape. Where's the stuff? I want to work on it today when we go to the library."

"It's in my bedroom, Emma, where are you going? The bus is here. Emma!"

But she was already sprinting back up the road towards Jude's house.

"What have you forgotten, then? You'd..." Mrs Hughes was saying as she opened the door. Then she stopped, surprised to find Emma, not Jude, standing out of breath at the top of the steps.

"Sorry to bother you, Mrs Hughes," Emma gasped. "Excuse me."

She was past her and taking the stairs two at a time. She burst into the bedroom and quickly scanned around. Nothing. Walls bare. Empty wastepaper basket. She spotted the folder on Jude's desk and swept it up.

Emma leapt back down the stairs, past Jude's bewildered mother and through the doorway, just in time to see the bus turning the corner, heading out of the village.

She'd missed it now but she didn't care. Jude could do what she liked. Emma hitched the bulky file under her arm. She was not giving up now. She was going on with the project.

When she got back to the bus stop, Jude was still standing there, arms folded, waiting for her.

"It was the rat-faced driver and he wouldn't wait. Sorry, Em. What shall we do now?"

"Try and scrounge a lift, I suppose. Or take the day off . . ."

Jude shook her head. "We can't do that."

Emma grinned. "Why not?"

Jude's reply was interrupted by a horn hooting. They both turned to see who it was: Ben Cooper in his dad's four-wheel drive. Stroke of luck him turning up, Emma thought as the door opened for them to get in, a genuine nineties knight in shining armour.

By the time they left the last few houses of the village behind, Ben and Jude were engrossed in murmured conversation. Emma fastened her seat belt and settled back in the rear passenger seat.

She'd known Ben for a long time. They had been in the same class in junior school. He'd certainly changed since those days. Emma pictured him then, aged about ten, tall and incredibly skinny. He had had really long hair for a boy, it stood out like a halo, a dandelion mass of curls. The other kids had teased him, said he only wore it like that to hide his ears. They still stuck out a bit, she noted, but his thick dark hair was clipped close to his head now, and even from the back you could tell he was good looking. She shifted slightly so she could see the rear-view mirror. He'd always had nice eyes, grey and wide apart. His eyebrows met above his nose, she'd never really noticed that before. Grecian. She moved again as he turned to say something to Jude. Went with the profile. She breathed in, nice aftershave. She couldn't quite place it, but it was expensive. She liked boys who had taste. The stuff most of them used could stun at twenty paces.

Ben laughed low at something Jude said and turned back to his driving. Emma watched her glancing over at him, and smiled. Jude couldn't keep her eyes off him. Obviously besotted. He was, too, by the look of it. Things had been moving on at a cracking pace. Emma was pleased for them and hoped it worked out. Ben was all right and he'd be a hell of a lot better off with Jude than with the appalling Caroline Grainger.

She stretched out on the back seat and closed her eyes. There was no jealousy. Emma just wondered what it would be like to fall for someone nice instead of totally untrustworthy Joe Thompson types.

The car, going over the traffic humps at the entrance to the car-park, jolted her awake. Emma immediately sensed that the atmosphere in the car had changed. It was now thick with tension.

"Look, Jude. I'm sorry, but I promised ages ago . . ." Ben's voice was strained, apologetic.

Emma sat up. What was this? Was she witnessing their first row?

Jude did not reply but continued to stare stonily out of the window.

They parked in uneasy silence. Jude was out of the car and striding away before the other two had unbuckled their seat belts.

Emma leant over and tapped Ben on the shoulder.

74

"Excuse me. But could you tell me what that was all about?"

Ben spread his hands helplessly, staring at Jude's retreating back.

"Search me," he said. "I just told her I couldn't take her to the party, Saturday night. I said I'd see her there and she blew me out. I've got to go early because I promised to help Malcolm, Caroline's brother, set up the sound equipment."

"What did she say?"

"She said, you'll be lucky."

Emma studied Ben's unhappy face in the rear-view mirror. Boys. Why don't they ever understand anything? It was important for Jude to be seen as his date, to be going out with him, not a "meet you later" kind of thing. How would he like to be stood up for a pile of disco equipment?

"I'll make sure she's there, don't worry," Emma said, touching his shoulder.

"Will you?"

"Yes, of course. I'm not a complete bitch," she grinned, "well, not all the time. I'll get her there but the rest is up to you."

"Thanks, Emma. I really like her, you know."

So do I, Emma thought, getting out of the car. And I wouldn't like to see her hurt. So you better not just be playing around with her, Ben Cooper.

Chapter 13

Emma selected SAVE from the command menu and punched the EXIT button. Miles Davis, turned way down, played softly on the stereo, otherwise there wasn't a sound. Outside the church clock struck once, twice. God, was that the time? She'd been at this for hours. She took off her glasses and closed her eyes, pinching the bridge of her nose. She pushed herself out of the pool of light coming from her desk-lamp and reached her arms up and back, trying to ease the aching stiffness in her shoulders.

She had been working hard ever since she got home. Her afternoon in the library had gone very well. One of the librarians had started chatting her up. Turned out he shared her passion for modern jazz. They'd talked a bit about that, and then, when she mentioned the Beresford case, he couldn't do enough. She'd noticed him before, but not his name. Simon Freeman, his lapel badge said, Library and Leisure Services.

"We're here to help" the logo asserted and he'd certainly done that. He'd found all sorts of stuff she would never have discovered, in parts of the library not open to the general public, including the typescript of talks given to a local history group, the Regional Crime Club, by Superintendent Jack Russell. He'd even photocopied it for her.

He'd been really nice. Not bad looking either. Thick streaky blond hair, well cut, falling over his eyes. Were they blue or grey? Blue, she decided. But not cold. Kind of sharp and bright. Intelligent. Good sense of humour. He was even better looking when he smiled, and he smiled a lot. Probably supposed to as part of the job. Nice clothes. Emma liked the wide navy braces over a very white shirt so much that she was thinking of getting some herself. Double cuffs, turned back, revealed a slim expensive watch and wide flat wrists covered in thick golden hair. How old? Twenties, maybe mid twenties, it wasn't all that old . . .

She stretched out her legs and let her head rest on the back of the chair. Her eyes closed and her glasses, dangling from her hand, fell to the ground. She wondered what he'd be like, and let herself drift for while in the cool, complex rhythms of modern jazz and the pleasures of fantasy.

Emma woke up to the monotonous thud, thud of the record still turning and rubbed her arms. It was cold now and she was stiffer than ever. She went to turn the stereo off and nearly trod on her glasses. She put them on, pushing them up her nose. They felt odd. She rarely wore them now, but this kind of close work made her eyes hurt if she kept in her contact lenses.

She had more than enough here for a grade A History project. All the information had been read and reread and everything was labelled now and correctly filed. The interview tapes had been meticulously transcribed, key statements marked in different-coloured highlighter pen, careful notes taken and all the events ordered and classi-fied. But she needed more if she was to stand a chance in that journalism competition. The newspaper cutting was in the centre of the charcoal-grey pinboard above her desk. Emma knew what it said by heart but she read it again.

> This competition is open to aspiring young journalists, aged 16–20. Entrants are invited to select a local event, or news story, and use their journalistic skills to give it wider interest.
>
> The panel of judges, all experienced journalists currently working for national newspapers, will be looking for freshness and originality. The winning entry will not rely on writing talent alone, but will be expected to show real insight into news values and an eye for a story.

The small print of the rules and conditions blurred as Emma continued to stare at the noticeboard. She needed more. But what? There was something. She'd missed something. Somewhere a dog barked and then a car started up. Sounds carried far at this time of night, it was so terribly quiet. She stripped off her clothes and fell into bed as the church clock struck three o'clock. Too tired to think about it now. Dad would be up soon to do the milking.

Extreme tiredness prevented the sleep she craved from coming easily. She drifted for a while and then her whole body jerked and she heard a voice, and saw a face, half dream, half reality.

Eileen Stanley leered towards her, eyes bulging, greedy with memory.

"Upstairs ... we went upstairs ... you know what I mean ... doing a bit of courting."

One eye winked and her pink-lipstick mouth opened wide in jeering laughter.

"People your age think you invented it, think you invented it . . ."

Her face faded but disembodied phrases from the conversation Emma had transcribed came and went, like voices on the wind.

" – their David . . . terrible state . . . terrible state. Old Ma Wyatt, not one to cross . . . Ask her. She knows. Knows about it."

Emma turned over, burying her head in the pillow, trying to block it out but the voice went on:

" – funny little kid . . .

. . . demon for dressing up. Shawls. Beads.

. . . Some of it quite expensive."

Then Eileen Stanley had gone and a woman's hand, thin and lean, wearing silver rings, held out a piece of lined A4 paper.

"I do remember something," Emma read. "She was wearing these beads . . ."

The rest of it made no sense, but she knew the handwriting. She was just working out whose it was when the page changed to typing. An old man read:

"It is quite common, in cases of this kind, for the perpetrator to take something belonging to the victim. A piece of clothing, perhaps, or jewellery. It is for this reason that information about certain items, found at the scene of the crime, was deliberately withheld . . ."

The voice faded out. This time she could see, further down the page, the words on the typewritten manuscript.

The exact nature of this unusual ligature was never made public . . .

Then she heard her own voice, reading from the dictionary.

"**Ligature,** *n.* & *v.t.* Thing used for tying or binding, especially, band or cord used to tie up . . . strangulation . . ."

Emma jerked from sleep, fighting for breath. Somehow the bed sheet had got twisted and tightened round her neck. She threw it away from her and lay back massaging her throat, trying to control her ragged breathing.

There was a soft, tentative knock at the door.

"Emma? Are you all right in there?"

It was her dad. Must have got up to do the milking.

"Yes, thanks," she managed to say.

"I was passing. Thought I heard you call out."

"Just a dream I was having."

"Want a cup of tea?"

"No, thanks," she said automatically, but then changed her mind. Her throat hurt abominably. She could hardly swallow. "Yes, please. I'll come down for it."

Her dad looked up as she came into the kitchen. He smiled to see her standing there, hair all stuck up on one side and her glasses on. His little girl again for a fleeting minute.

"Here you are, then." He handed her a steaming mug. "Haven't seen you in those for a long time."

She pushed the glasses up her nose and yawned as she sat down.

"Bit too early in the morning for contact lenses."

"What's up? Bad dream?"

She shrugged. "Something like that."

"Want to tell me about it?"

She put her hands round her mug and stared into it.

"It wasn't a dream, exactly . . ." Then she looked up at him and smiled. "I can hardly remember it."

"OK now?" he said, reaching over.

She nodded and took his hand. The plain gold wedding ring contrasted against the brown of his skin and the palm was rough with calluses. They did not talk much. Never did. But when she was little she had followed him round all the time, wanting to be a farmer just like him, and even now, at moments like this, she found his presence hugely comforting.

"I'm fine. Dad. Honest."

"Right then." He drained his tea in one long gulp. "Better get on. You go back to bed now. I'll tell Mum to let you have a lie-in. You look as though you need it."

Chapter 14

Emma woke suddenly, sensing it was late. The sun was streaming through a gap where the curtains didn't quite close. She squinted at the digital alarm, 11:30, and stumbled out of bed, heading for the shower. Deep, dreamless sleep, after her late night and fractured dreams, had left her feeling dazed and groggy.

She stood in the shower for a long time, letting the water stream over her, and dressed slowly before going downstairs in search of coffee.

"Oh, hello. How are you feeling?"

Marion Tasker smiled as her daughter came in, immaculately dressed all in black, her wet hair slicked severely back, and in those boots that made her a good head and shoulders taller than her mother.

"I'm fine, Mum, thanks. Any chance of a cup of coffee?"

"Jude phoned," Marion said as she poured boiling water into the filter, "but said not to disturb you, she'd ring later. Oh, and a young man called from the library. You haven't forgotten to take your books back again, have you? You know how the fines mount up . . ."

"I was going to take them in today, so you don't have to nag. Did he give his name? What did he say?"

Her mother filled a cup and handed it to her.

"Yes, he did. Simon something. Just asked if you were there and could he speak to you, and when I said you

82

weren't available he thanked me and rang off. I thought it was a bit odd, I mean, they don't usually ring people up at home, do they? What do you think he wanted?"

"I have no idea." Emma drank her coffee and cast about for a change of subject. "There was something I meant to ask you," she said after a moment or two. "You know David Wyatt? Did he have a brother called Robbie?"

Her mother thought for a minute.

"Yes, he did, as a matter of fact. He was killed in a motor-cycle accident."

"When was that?"

"Oh, a long time ago. Back in the seventies. His family were very cut up, especially David. They were pretty close, I seem to remember. Why are you so interested?"

"Oh, nothing. Something someone said. Just curiosity." Emma finished her coffee and picked up her bag.

"I'm off now. See you later." She leant over and kissed her on the cheek. "Did anyone tell you? You're a terrific mother."

"Emma!" her mother shouted, just as the front door slammed. "You've forgotten your library books."

But it was too late. Marion Tasker squared the books on the hall table and made a mental note to take them in herself, first thing Monday morning.

Emma waited patiently at the enquiry desk until she was at the front of the queue.

"How can I help you?" he said, without looking up.

"I need a new library ticket."

"Lost?"

"Yes."

83

His hand reached for the appropriate form.

"That'll be thirty pence. Name?"

"Emma Tasker. T-A-S-K-E-R."

He looked up and smiled. She'd remembered right, his eyes were blue.

"Sorry," he said to the person behind her, hooking his coat off the back of the chair. "This position is closed. Perhaps one of my colleagues can help you."

"Would you like some lunch?" he asked when they were outside.

"Um, yes. Fine," Emma said, surprised.

She hadn't quite expected this but she was not going to pass it up. She hadn't even had breakfast yet and she was absolutely starving.

"Where shall we go?"

Emma shrugged and shook her head. "I don't know. Wherever."

He took her arm, guiding her through the Saturday shoppers.

"Come on then, there's a great little place round the corner."

The café was crowded but they found a table near the back.

"Have you been here before?" he asked as he studied the menu.

"Well, yes . . ."

"Hi, Emma," the waitress said as she came up, eyes asking, "Who's the guy?" over her order pad. "Are you ready to order, sir?"

"Er, yes. I think I'll have the lasagne."

The girl wrote it down.

"Madam?" she enquired, eyebrows quirking higher.

"Me too," Emma replied.

"Anything to drink?"

"I'll have a beer, please. Beck's," Simon said. "How about you?"

"Perrier."

"Would that be with ice and lemon?"

"Yes, thanks. With ice and lemon." Emma's words were clipped.

"OK," the waitress grinned, "be right with you."

"Do you know her?"

"Yes, she goes to my school. They do too."

She nodded towards where the waitress stood with two of the cooks who had come out of the back to nudge and giggle with each other.

"Always the same in a small town."

Emma sighed. "Tell me about it."

"Why did you phone me?" Emma asked.

"Because I wanted to see you again, isn't that obvious?"

Emma laughed. "No. Really."

"Of course, really."

Emma laughed again. "How did you get my number?"

He wiped the foam from his mouth with the back of his hand.

"Looked you up on the computer and there you were. Name, address, telephone number, two books overdue and two fines still outstanding."

"How long have you worked there," she asked as the food came, "at the library."

"Well, I don't exactly work there. Not strictly. I'm a student."

Emma quickly revised her estimation of his age downwards. Student was OK. Even Dad would buy "student".

Not that she cared all that much but after the fuss they'd made about Joe, she could do without the hassle.

"What kind of student?"

"What kind do you think?" he said, laughing. "A library student. I'm here on work placement. But I'm really interested in archive work . . ."

She regarded him over a forkful of food. Surely he wasn't going to start talking about that? It sounded deadly. If he was, she'd have to think again. No matter how good looking they were, Emma couldn't stand guys who bored her.

"What I really want to do is . . ." Then he broke off, "Just kidding. Everyone else finds it really tedious so I don't talk about it."

"So, what did you want to see me about?"

"Well," he wiped his mouth, "I really did want to see you again, but you're right, I do have another motive." He put his fork down and pushed away the plate of food. "You see, your project interests me." He paused and leant forward. "I – I don't quite know how to put this, but the fact is . . ." He looked away from her for a second or two before going on, ". . . the fact is, my mother's name was Beresford before she married my dad. So that kind of makes me Jenny's brother."

Emma's large bite of the microwaved lasagne stuck like a lump of molten lead in her throat. She started to choke.

"Are you OK?" He leant over, blue eyes full of concern, and delivered a sharp blow to the centre of her back before handing her drink to her.

She gulped the water gratefully and, when she had recovered sufficiently, apologized to him.

"Why should you be sorry?" he replied. "She died before I was born. I never even knew her. It wasn't till I was quite old that I even knew she existed. My mother never talked about that time in her life. Doesn't now. It's like the time she married my dad is Year Zero. Nothing before that is ever spoken about."

"So how did you find out?"

"I found a photograph. I must have been about seven. I was looking for something in a book and this photo dropped out. I remember staring at it, wondering what it was doing there. I'd never seen it before and I wanted to know who the children were. They weren't cousins or anyone I knew. They were complete strangers. So I asked my dad about it. He went white and there was this terrible stretching silence. I was really scared. I thought he was mad at me and I didn't know what I could have possibly done to make him so angry. Then he told me. He didn't know about the other two, but the one in the middle was Jenny. Then he called my mother in. That's the only time they spoke about it."

"Ever?"

"Yes. My mum got – in a very bad way after Jenny's death and she's had problems since. Spells of depression that last for weeks, months even. When you live with someone like that you grow up avoiding anything that might start them off. You ... you get very protective towards them . . ."

His voice trailed off. A muscle jumped in his cheek and a quick reflex frown contracted his high forehead.

"Why did she keep it? The photograph, I mean. If what happened to Jenny upset her so much that she wanted to erase that whole part of her life," Emma shook out the napkin to wipe her mouth, "why keep reminders?"

Simon shrugged. "I really don't know. She got rid of everything else. But maybe she had to keep something.

Even though she had to hide it away, I don't think she could bear to get rid of it altogether. It was taken at the fête on the day Jenny died. She'd won the fancy-dress competition or something. Her face is full of joy, she looks so happy."

"Coffee? Dessert?" The waitress was back, clearing the table. "I hope you enjoyed your meal."

"Not for me," Simon said. "Do you want anything?"

"Er, yes. Coffee, please. Espresso."

"OK, make that two." He looked at his watch. "I should be getting back, but I'm sure they can cope without me."

"Did you come here, to this town, deliberately?" Emma asked after the coffee arrived. "I mean, to find out about what happened to Jenny?"

"Well, not deliberately, not entirely." He took a sip but it was too hot. He put down his cup. "It just occurred to me when I saw the name on the placement list. I suddenly wanted to know more about where my mother had been at that time in her life and – what had happened." He grinned and laughed rather nervously. "Kind of a weird idea, huh? Researching your own mother."

Emma nodded her agreement but didn't say anything. After a moment or two he went on.

"You know, it's strange. I hardly know you but I'm telling you things I've never told anyone in my entire life. That's odd, don't you think?"

Emma shrugged and stirred her coffee.

He leant towards her. "I'm going to tell you something I've never told a living soul. My dad was going to throw that photograph out, burn it. But before he could, I took it. I was an only child. Are you an only child, Emma?"

"No," she shook her head. "I have two younger brothers."

"Well, I was. And kind of lonely, I suppose, because sometimes – after I found the photograph – I'd go and get it out. First I'd check that no one was in the house and then I'd take it out and stare at it for hours. I . . ." He hesitated, as though regretting his decision to confide in her, and then went on. "I used to pretend they came out of the picture and played with me in their fancy dress clothes, and I'd feel proud and special, like I had a real live sister."

"Weren't you scared?" Emma asked. "I think I would have been. Didn't she seem like a ghost?"

There was something peculiar about the image he had presented to her. Macabre even. Creepy.

"No," he looked up in surprise, "that never occurred to me. Well, it did. To be honest, it was part of the game. But I was never frightened by it. It was a different feeling altogether. You see, in the games she was safe. I saved her. Even the beads . . ."

"Beads?" Emma said sharply. "What beads?"

"In the picture she's wearing these beads. She was wearing them when she was killed. Didn't you know? She was almost strangled by them."

She thought her way back through the case. No mention of beads, except . . . Of course! The unusual nature of the ligature.

"These beads," she asked. "What did they look like? Do you remember at all?"

"Well, they were this shape." He began drawing on the tablecloth with a clean, well-manicured fingernail. "And about this size. They looked heavy on a child's neck, you know?"

"What colour were they? Could you see?"

"A kind of milky green. Looked like glass. Tiny dots of other colours, red and blue, in little squirls."

"How do you remember so clearly, just from a photograph?"

Emma stared at him, frowning, trying to recall something herself. Somewhere she'd seen beads like that, but she couldn't place where or when. She pinched the bridge of her nose. Her brain was rapidly reaching overload.

"I told you," he said as he called for the bill. "I used to study it. Going over it, sometimes for hours, with my dad's magnifying glass."

"I've got to get back," he said when they were outside. "but . . ."

He pushed his hair out of his eyes and looked down at her. He was tall, about six feet. His grey-blue eyes had a slightly pleading, uncertain look. Her heart skipped a beat. What if he asked for a date? What would she do? What would she do if he didn't?

"But what?"

"There's something I meant to ask you. A favour. Can I see you again? I can't really explain, standing here on the pavement."

"Yes, I mean, OK. I don't see why not."

Emma was pleased and more than a little intrigued, but it wouldn't do to sound too eager.

He stared down at the ground, hands thrust deep in his pockets.

"How about tonight?" he said after a pause.

"Tonight?" She hadn't expected it to be as soon as that and was just about to say yes when she remembered the party. "Oh, no. I can't. Maybe some other time. Thanks – thanks for lunch."

His half-smile showed it was the answer he'd expected. A girl like her was bound to have a boyfriend.

"I'm going to a party," Emma explained. "I'd ask you to come but it's an eighteenth. Invites only."

"Where?"

"At the Grange. But tell you what . . ." Emma frowned in thought, and then her face cleared. "Why don't you meet me in the bar?"

Simon smiled. "Fine. What time?"

"Around nine?"

"Sounds good to me." He leant towards her, his lips brushing her cheek. "See you there, Emma."

Chapter 15

"Hello, Emma. She's upstairs."

Emma knew there was something wrong as soon as Mrs Hughes opened the door.

"Is that your mum in the car?" Jude's mother peered past her. "You'd better ask her to come in for a minute."

Emma beckoned for her mother to come inside and ran up the stairs as fast as her short skirt and high heels allowed. She found Jude still in her old jeans and sweatshirt.

"I'm not going,' she said, without looking up from her magazine.

"Oh, yes you are."

"No, I'm not." Jude flicked over a couple of pages. "You go on your own."

Emma hitched her skirt above her thigh and knelt down with some difficulty.

"What's the matter?"

"Ben and Caroline. They'll be together. Like Mrs Stanley said, they're made for each other," Jude muttered into the threadbare knees of her jeans. "I reckon I was only invited so I could be humiliated."

Emma rolled her eyes and tried to curb her impatience.

"I really don't think so, Jude. Ben's nuts about you, anyone can see that. Come on, you've got to get ready."

Jude shook Emma's hand off and began picking out threads from fraying edges.

"I told you, I'm not going."

Emma stood up. "I promised Ben you'd be there and he'll be waiting. And if you don't go," she said, smoothing wrinkles out of her dress, "they'll be back together by the end of the evening, you can guarantee it. So get up off the floor. I can't kneel down any longer. My tights are bagging."

"I haven't got anything to wear," Jude said, not looking at her friend standing there in black high heels, long legs in sheer, black, fine-denier tights and spray-on Lycra dress. "I won't feel right if I do go." Jude looked around in despair. "Whatever I wear, I'll look a mess and you look fantastic."

"Oh, pull yourself together and stop being so pathetic," Emma said impatiently, holding out a hand to pull her up. "I'll sort something out while you're in the shower. Now get going. And don't have the water too hot," Emma shouted after her, "or you'll get the fresh-boiled lobster effect. I'll tell Mum to have another cup of coffee."

Jude dutifully turned the temperature down and stepped under the shower.

Emma was right. It would be cowardly not to go and she knew, whatever she pretended, that Ben would be waiting, would be hurt if she didn't show up. Maybe it was her he wanted. Maybe. She wanted him. She had never wanted anyone or anything as much as this. She felt confused inside; beaten up and bruised by new emotions. For the last few days she had thought of nothing else – seeing his face, talking to him endlessly in her mind – but when they were together there always seemed too much or too little to say, so that she either found herself tongue-tied or chattering on like an airhead. Compared to Ben, all the boys she'd known before were so many forgotten names scrawled on scruffy folders.

It was easier not to go tonight. That way she couldn't get hurt. Couldn't make a fool of herself. Something as sudden as this could prove to be as insubstantial as the bubbles foaming down and swirling around her feet. She closed her eyes and threw her head back, her sodden blond hair falling dark and heavy on to her shoulders. The full force of the water hit her in the face as she followed the tangled lines of logic that had led to her decision to miss the party.

There was another, deeper reason. She felt out of control, helplessly slipping and sliding into something so absolutely new, it was frightening. Not going tonight was the last chance to climb back, the last handhold. She soaped herself with the shower gel. The clean, sharp sandalwood perfume smelt of visits to her grandmother, of childhood.

"I can't wear that!"

Jude entered the bedroom towelling her hair, and regarded the dress Emma had picked out for her with horror.

"Why not? It'll look terrific."

Jude picked the dress up. The sequins on the bodice shimmered as it slid off the bed. The black crêpe de Chine was so fine it felt weightless. Held up by a prayer and two thin straps, she remembered the thrill when she'd found it: an original sixties little black evening dress.

"It's too short." Beautifully cut, it fell into graceful

lines as she held it up. "And it's backless. And practically frontless!"

"Exactly!" Emma exclaimed in triumph. "If you've got it, flaunt it, that's what I say. I don't know why you buy these things if you aren't going to wear them."

"I know you don't," Jude replied. "I buy them because I want them – like a collection. Some of them aren't even my size."

Emma took the dress and held it against her.

"Well, this one is. So get it on."

"What about shoes? And tights? I mean, I need a whole outfit to go with that."

"You ought to wear stockings really," Emma regarded the dress critically, "but you'll have to make do with my spare tights. I found these black patent platforms and this little evening bag. You've got more stuff in your cupboards than the average wardrobe department."

"Oh, OK, then."

Emma grinned. Jude's reluctance was less convincing now. She was beginning to find the idea attractive.

"What are you doing?" Jude said as she applied a second layer of mascara.

In the mirror she could see Emma going through the beads and necklaces that hung from a frame on the opposite side of the room.

"Just looking for something."

"What? You're already wearing a choker."

"That necklace you made. You know, the one with the green glass beads."

Jude twirled the mascara wand, trying to avoid getting it in her eyes.

"What for? You can't wear it with that dress, it wouldn't look right. Stick to the choker is my advice."

"I wasn't going to wear them. I was going to show them to someone."

"Who?"

Jude started on the other eye. Emma was right about the shadows she'd said to use. The different hues gave her eyes a deeper, almost violet shade of blue.

"This guy I met . . ."

"What guy? Where did you meet him?"

"At the library. He took me out to lunch and I'm meeting him this evening – at the hotel."

Jude swivelled round. She couldn't concentrate on dramatic revelations and applying mascara as well.

"Let me get this straight, Emma." Jude's look of amused surprise was emphasised by one eye being made up more heavily than the other. "You've got a date tonight with someone you picked up in the *library?* I thought that only happened in *My Guy* photostories!"

"Well, I didn't exactly pick him up . . . His name's Simon. He was helping me on Friday."

Jude turned back to her mascara.

"Oh yeah, I remember. The nice-looking one who isn't bald and over fifty. Anyway, the necklace isn't there any more. I sold it to Mr Wyatt. So there's no point looking for it."

"What?"

Jude's hand jerked at Emma's shouted astonishment and she gave herself an extra eyebrow.

"Damn!" she muttered, groping for the tissues and make-up remover. "Yeah. Said he was looking for something unusual for his wife's birthday. Not bad, eh?" She blinked in satisfaction, smiling at her face in reflection. "He gave me twenty quid for it."

"Oh, no. You have to be joking. Please, tell me you're kidding."

The multicoloured strands of beads slithered through Emma's hands and skittered against each other. What did Wyatt want them for? A chill crept up the back of her neck. Emma had met his wife. She was strictly thin gold chains and Cartier copies.

"What's the big deal?" Jude asked, puzzled by Emma's reaction. "What's so important about a string of beads?"

"The thing is – I don't think they are just any old beads. I think they might be . . ."

A knock on the door cut off the rest of what Emma was going to say. It was Jude's mother reminding them that if they didn't hurry up they stood a very good chance of being late for Caroline's next birthday party, never mind this one.

Chapter 16

The place was filling up. Clare Conrad looked at her watch, wondering when it would be decently possible to leave. Emma and Jude gave her a wave as they drifted past on their way to greet the birthday girl. They looked great, but in the wrong place. Like they were out clubbing and had somehow ended up in the pompous function rooms of country hotel by mistake.

"What's so funny?" David Wyatt asked.

"Oh, nothing," Clare said, sipping her drink.

Dave drained his glass and took another from the tray of a passing waitress. He downed that in seconds and was looking round again, greedy for more. Clare wondered how long he'd been drinking like this. She wondered what he was doing here at all, for that matter. He'd hardly been in school all week. Caroline Grainger's mother seemed to have invited everyone who played the slightest part in her daughter's life, from her music teacher to the vicar. Clare could see a scattering of younger staff from school, attracted, no doubt, by the prospect of free booze and all that food.

"What are you doing here?" he suddenly asked, as if he could read her mind. "Wouldn't have thought this was exactly your scene."

"Caroline's mother and I are cousins, and I didn't have anything else on. I don't intend to stay long but I thought I'd better put in an appearance." She glanced around at the opulent surroundings, the groaning buffet table, the waitresses gliding about with different trays. This must be costing a packet. "Represent the poor relations, that kind of thing."

"Heard from Ali recently?" he said through a mouthful of canapé.

"Yes, she phoned last week."

"Haven't seen her since Mum's funeral . . ."

"Well, she's been very busy," Clare said quickly to fill the awkward silence.

"These days we hardly ever see her. I thought she might fit us into her schedule over Easter. Did she mention anything?"

Clare looked away, not quite knowing what to say. It was always like this when they spoke about his sister. His eyes, behind the glasses, were exactly the same colour as Ali's and contained a special kind of puzzled pleading which contrasted with his sarcasm and habitual bitterness.

"Do you fancy a real drink?" He grimaced. "This stuff is never champagne. Tastes like flat lemonade."

Clare followed him into the hotel bar. He ordered two gin and tonics and settled himself on a stool.

"Well," he said, "what did she say?"

"Oh, you know. Like I said, she's been very busy. You know the sort of job she's got. The pressures she's under . . ."

"Oh, yes. The famous job." He laughed into his first draught from the glass. "I don't know how she can involve herself in trash like that. Talk about selling out . . ."

Clare sighed as he talked on, only half listening. Why did he have to put on this act? Underneath it all, he was incredibly proud of Ali. And she adored him, always had. She'd hero-worshipped him as a child and followed in his footsteps through school to university. Was he jealous because Ali had achieved more than he had? That would be the most obvious explanation but Clare didn't think that was the reason at all. It was rather that, somehow, David's view of her had become distorted and fissured by the fault lines of his own pessimism and depression. That was why Ali wouldn't go and see him, preferring to avoid the constant needling and sniping that went on whenever they were together.

"Perhaps she believes in it," Clare said suddenly.

"What?" He turned, the sweet scent of gin sickly on his breath.

"Perhaps she thinks she can do some good. No point in having a watchdog programme nobody watches." She looked at him, head on one side. "You should be pleased for her that it's so popular, David. Thanks for the drink. See you at school."

Clare got up, leaving her drink practically untouched. She wanted to go now; she'd had enough.

She walked through the bar towards the swing doors that led to the hotel foyer. Emma Tasker waved from one of the window alcoves and then returned her attention to her companion. Clare had seen her in the mirror at the bar, sitting behind what looked like a large vodka and tonic, deep in animated conversation with a young man she had never seen before. What was she doing out here with the grown-ups? She should be in the party. By the sound of things the disco had started. Clare shrugged and went in search of someone to order her a taxi. Par for that particular course. She'd never known Emma do what was expected.

*

"Yes," Emma was saying, "absolutely no problem."

"Are you sure?" Simon asked.

"See that woman over there?" She nodded towards Clare making for the door. "She'd be able to tell you in a flash."

Simon had always wanted to know who the other two children were in the Jenny photograph. When he had first found it, his father had shaken his head in silent warning not to ask. Then it became impossible. He'd been left to puzzle alone over who they might be. It was not so much the little girl. He'd felt drawn to the older one, standing taller than his sister and slightly behind her, an arm resting on her shoulder. The Pirate. In the furtive fantasy games played out in his parents' quiet suburban house, this figure took on roles to rival his own when it came to saving Jenny. These childhood obsessions were still in his adult mind and provided part of his real motive for seeking to discover exactly what had happened to his sister.

"Thanks, Emma."

"I'd be happy to ask her. You haven't got the photo with you, by any chance?"

"No, I left it at home. To be honest, I didn't think I'd ever be able to talk to anyone about it."

"Why not?"

"I don't know."

There was an awkward pause. He put his hands in his pockets and stared at the table. He couldn't tell her. It would sound too weird, and maybe it was. Sometimes he had a hard time explaining to himself why he felt like this.

"Are you sorry you asked me?" Emma asked eventually.

"No, not at all . . ."

"Good, because I've got my own reasons for wanting to see that photograph."

"Oh." He was suddenly intrigued. "Like what?"

"The beads. You know, the ones you described your sister wearing? As you were talking, I was thinking, 'I've seen them.' And then, on the bus, going home, it came to me. They sound just like some beads Jude bought..."

Her hair shone in the brightly lit bar, her dark eyes glowed with excitement and her pale face was flushed with colour along each cheekbone. She crossed her legs and leant towards him. He was beginning to enjoy being with her.

"Who's Jude?" he asked.

"She's my friend. She's here. In the party. With her boyfriend, Ben."

"Where did she get them?"

"She bought them in Ben's dad's place. It's an antique shop. Well, it's a junk shop really..."

"Are you sure they are the same ones?"

"No," Emma frowned, "I mean they sound the same or ... or very similar," her slim expressive hands described her frustration, "but there's no way of positively identifying them – without the photograph." She turned her glass, moving the ice round and round. "I thought, if you lent it to me, I could enlarge it and then we might be able to tell if they are the same ones."

She looked at him, her large, dark eyes appealing for his help. She wanted something too. Well, who didn't? And what she'd said was interesting, to say the least ...

"Why not? You can blow it up poster-size if that's what you want."

"I knew you'd say yes." Emma's serious expression

was suddenly transformed by a dazzling smile. "Thanks, Simon."

He sat back and looked at her. She had it all worked out, her own options covered. She was clever all right and prepared to use her charms including her physical attractiveness, to manipulate and persuade. She was either excessively curious or extremely calculating. Perhaps both. And very impulsive. Any of the former traits could take her very far, especially as she'd told him she wanted to be a journalist, but the latter one could lead to disaster. She had the right stuff, but she really should be more careful about how she used it.

He folded his arms, considering. Whatever her motives, what she proposed suited his purpose. Besides, he smiled to himself, she was by far the most interesting person he'd met in his time in this small country town. He'd better be careful. Although she was younger than she looked, she was very attractive.

"OK. Say I get the photograph tomorrow. Have you got the beads? Have you told your friend about this?"

"Well," Emma bit her lip, "not exactly . . ."

"Not exactly what? You haven't exactly got the beads? Or you haven't told your friend about them?"

"Not exactly either. I didn't tell her because . . . I don't know, there wasn't time, and then I found out she'd sold them."

"What!" He drained the rest of his pint. "For Christ's sake, Emma! You spin me a story about how important your friend's beads are and then you tell me she's sold them! I can't cope with this without another drink. You want one?"

Emma nodded. She needed time to think. Jude selling the beads to Wyatt was a development she had not antici-

103

pated but it didn't have to mean the end. She was already hatching a plan to get them back, and Simon was going to let her copy the photograph anyway, so what was there to worry about?

"Who did she sell them to?" Simon asked when he returned. "Can you get them back?"

Emma bent towards him and lowered her voice.

"She sold them to that guy sitting at the bar . . ."

"Which guy? Where?" Simon asked, scanning the bar with new curiosity.

"Near where you were just now. Thinning hair, glasses, grey jacket. He's a teacher at our school. Don't look!" she added in an urgent whisper.

But of course he did. David Wyatt, who had been watching them in the mirror tiles behind the bar, saw him do it.

David Wyatt loosened his tie and undid the button of his shirt collar. Christ, it was hot. The place was filling, the bar becoming more crowded as the evening got into full swing. He wanted to filter out the voices and laughter around him and just concentrate on what those two were saying, but he was too far away. He couldn't move nearer without attracting their attention further. And they were already watching and talking about him. He knew it.

His head ached unbearably. The growing babble and chatter was making it worse and behind it, like the beating of his blood, was the constant thudding bass from that sodding awful party. He wanted to go somewhere quiet, but he could not leave. He had to stay and watch them watching him.

Emma Tasker. What was she doing in here? He

wouldn't trust her as far as he could throw her. And who was that guy with her? He seemed vaguely familiar. David searched his mind for possibilities and then the penny dropped. He nearly dropped his glass. Of course! He was a reporter. That was it. From the local rag. She had nagged and nagged last year for a work placement there. It was all coming back now. She wanted to be a journalist just like his bloody sister. He smiled to himself, but in the mirror it looked more like a snarl.

There was something else. Clare Conrad had told him about it just last week. He searched through the tangling webs of his recent memory. He hadn't been paying too much attention. Something about Emma going in for a competition. By Christ! His eyes narrowed but he looked away from his own reflection. It was getting hard to recognize the face he kept seeing there.

He could see straight through her. Like a pane of glass, like cellophane. She'd hi-jacked that project and was adding her own extra special twist to get it into the papers: "Love Child Killing – New Leads Discovered By Local Seventeen-Year-Old". The scheming, conniving little bitch! Well, he was on to her now. That was definitely worth another drink.

He reached in his pocket for change and the beads twisted themselves around his hand, holding it there. He threw a note on the bar and ordered a double.

David Wyatt stayed until he could hardly stand, the gin he steadily consumed serving to feed, rather than curb, his growing paranoia.

Chapter 17

Even in the dream, Clare was residually aware that she was in school and she resented it. Dreaming about school was boring; it was a dream wasted. And this one was worse than most. The bell rang on and on, all break and dinner-time, all through every lesson. She was just about to add her own scream to the maddening insistent noise when she woke up to the ringing of the telephone.

She leant over and groped about, trying to locate it. A pile of books and papers slid off the night stand on to the floor. Who the hell could be phoning? It was four o'clock in the morning. She picked up the receiver and threw herself back on the pillow.

"Hello. Clare Conrad."

The silence that followed went on long enough for Clare to think she'd got a breather and then a voice said,

"It's me. It's Ali."

Clare closed her eyes. Of course. Who else would phone at this hour?

"Ali. Do you know what time it is?"

There was another pause. A lighter clicked and Ali exhaled. So she was smoking again.

"Not exactly. I'm not wearing a watch and can't see a clock but I'd guess it to be about four o'clock."

"Spot on. What do you want?"

"I couldn't sleep . . ."

"And you're making sure I don't either . . ."

"I had to talk to someone. I . . . I . . ."

Ali's voice trailed off but something told Clare not to interrupt the silence that followed.

"I've been having therapy . . ."

"Why? How long for?" Clare asked.

She pressed the receiver closer to her ear. She was having difficulty picking up what Ali said. Her voice sounded strange, the words soft and slurred.

"For some time. You remember that panic attack I had in the cinema? Well, it happened again. A couple of times. More than a couple of times. It was developing into a real phobia. Interfering in my work. Someone, a friend, thought it might be stress-related – something similar had happened to him and he . . . he recommended this woman. She's really good . . ."

Clare thought back to the incident in the cinema. Ali had come up for the weekend and they'd gone to see a film at the local arts centre. They were late. The film was just starting and the only remaining seats were at the front. Halfway down the stairs, the lights had gone down. Clare had stopped, waiting for their eyes to adjust to the sudden darkness, before continuing down the stairs. When she turned to say something, there was no one there. Ali had not moved. Clare had gone back and taken her arm. Her skin was clammy, she was trembling. Clare thought she was going to pass out. Two attendants had to help get her outside. Clare remembered their embarrassed distaste at Ali throwing up into a concrete wastepaper bin.

At the time they thought it was something she ate or some kind of bug. Now it turned out it was a full-blown panic attack. The first of many, according to what Ali was saying, brought on by sudden transitions of light to dark, or dark to light.

". . . she says it's not strictly photophobia or achluophobia. It's kind of a combination of both."

"It's not what?" Clare interrupted. "Photo is light – I understand that. But I've never heard of the other one . . ."

"Abnormal fear of darkness."

"Oh, right."

Clare closed her eyes. By now Ali would have read every available book on phobias, anxiety, panic attacks, and would know enough to write a thesis on the subject. She had always been like that; for her, appropriating facts was the only proper route to understanding.

"This woman. Your therapist. What does she think is causing this thing that's happening to you? Is it stress, or what?"

"Stress acts as a trigger. It's not a causal factor . . ."

"So what is?"

"Some kind of trauma."

"What kind of trauma?"

"I don't know, do I? Hence the therapist. She uses dreams . . ." Ali's voice suddenly clotted with unspoken emotions. "I have to keep – I'm keeping this dream diary . . ."

That's why you're phoning me now, Ali, Clare thought. You can't sleep, can you? Because you'll dream if you do. You're taking pills, or drinking, or both, I can tell by the slur in your voice. Anything to stop yourself dreaming.

"Clare. Are you still there?"

"Yes." Clare's voice softened, "I'm still here. Look, Ali – talking on the phone, it's not getting us anywhere. When can you come up?"

"I thought Tuesday. Evening train."

"That's good. Let me know which one. I'll meet you."

"Thanks, Clare."

"That's OK. See you soon. Take care, Ali."

She thought she detected dawn streaking the far horizon but could not be sure. The constant glow of city light made it hard to tell the movement of night to morning.

Alison Wyatt had found out everything about her condition. At first it had helped to know that it was relatively common, so she was not going crazy. She was not alone, lots of people suffered like her in varying degrees. Phobias were treatable, her therapist had explained, and could often be traced back to some seemingly trivial childhood incident.

Ali had not been able to recall anything to her conscious mind that could possibly account for this growing disruption in her adult life.

"It doesn't mean to say there's nothing there." The therapist had smiled patiently. "It's just hidden. Locked in. We have to discover it, and you must relive it, if you are to be really free . . ."

That's where the dreams came in.

Keeping the dream diary had been hard at first. Ali knew she must dream, everybody did. It was a normal part of every night's sleep. But she could not remember.

So she had to train herself to wake up, lie still in the moments between sleep and wakefulness remembering the dream, and then write it down.

Ali flicked through the notebook she used as a diary. At first only fragments came back; stupid little things from everyday life, that seemed of no significance, no importance. Ali was becoming impatient with the whole process when she began to notice a pattern, a recurrence.

109

It was the place. Always the same place. Gradually, as she became familiar with the technique, she recalled more and more.

At first, Ali had shared her therapist's excitement, conscientious in recording every detail.

She turned to an entry, a week or so after her mother's funeral.

22nd November 2.15 a.m.
I am in the place again. I am in the doorway. I don't know if I am an adult or child. I can't see myself and have no way of knowing. Inside is very dark, no windows, but light breaks through gaps in the roof and shines down, almost solid with floating dust, tiger striping the cluttered interior. The walls are rough and the floor is stamped-down earth. There is a thin chemical smell, like weedkiller, and something more pungent, creosote? And something else, more organic, seems to catch in the back of my throat. Immediately I can't breathe and I can't move. I feel trapped and helpless, I am starting to panic. There is something in there, over in the corner, moving. It's alive, I can see by it's eyes shining. It knows I'm there and I'm still frozen. It's coming towards me. It's mouth, opening and shutting.

The entry stopped abruptly at the point where Ali had woken up.

She turned the pages of the diary to the most recent ones.

3rd March 5.15 a.m.

The same place. The same feeling. Everything the same. Except now I have something in my hand. Flowers, I think. I can smell them and feel the hard green knobbly stems in my fist. But as I stand at the door I squeeze and squeeze them until they disintegrate and turn to slime which oozes through my fingers.

7th March 6.10 a.m.

The mouth is not going to eat me. It is talking to me. I know the voice and understand. I move and I step out of the place but the light is blinding. It goes like a laser, right into me through my eyes, cauterizing my mind so I remember nothing.

That was the last entry Ali had made. It was getting too close. She felt the dreams beating on the drum of memory. The skin, like an opaque membrane, was stretched taut now and thinning, ready to split and reveal the past and the nightmare beneath.

She told herself it was pressure of work that led her to cancel her next two appointments but, so far, each time her therapist phoned her, she'd failed to make an answering call.

Chapter 18

When dawn finally came it was pale and unspectacular. David Wyatt woke to another terrible hangover. He was chilled to the marrow but sweat broke out on his face and over his chest. He couldn't stop shaking.

Grey light filtered through the trees. The mounting birdsong screamed in his head like a jet engine. How did he get here? He opened the car window to let out some of the fetid air. He had no idea. Images of the night before came back in bizarre fragments, in an order which made no sense, like the scattered pieces of a jigsaw puzzle.

He glanced in the rear-view mirror. They weren't there now – had gone home long ago – but he could see the marks the big four-wheel drive had left in the mud by the side of the track. It had been Ben Cooper and Jude Hughes parked there, he'd recognized them.

He leant forward, put his head on the steering wheel and shut his eyes, trying to squeeze out the memory of what he had done, but he couldn't. He saw himself getting out of his car, even drunk he could still move in the woods without making a sound. He'd gone over and stood, at a point where he could see but not be seen, and watched them. He'd stayed, unable to tear himself away. Black dress, white flesh, tumbling long golden hair; the images played back on the inner screen of his mind.

He'd never done anything remotely like that before. What was happening to him? Acting like some dirty old man. His stomach churned. Last night's gin bubbled up, tasting like stale cologne, filling the back of his throat. He threw the car door open just in time and vomited.

He felt better then, emptied of some of the poisons within, but he was in no condition to drive. He made his way shakily to his mother's house and let himself in. He'd brought a sleeping bag up last week, and a camping stove and coffee. He'd told Elizabeth it was to keep an eye on the place, minimize the risk of vandalism. She'd given him one of her looks but hadn't said anything. He gave a silent prayer to whatever gods had inspired him. Now he could come and go as he liked and always have a cover story.

Chapter 19

"I'm going up Mitre to take some pics. Do you want to come?" Emma stood kicking at the gravel on the path, camera slung round her neck. "It's a lovely morning."

Jude squinted round the door, feet cold on the tiled hall floor, trying to think. A brisk walk wasn't what she had in mind, even if the sun was shining. She was still in her nightdress and only half awake. All she wanted to do was go back to sleep. On the other hand, her mother, clattering about at the back of the house, was still annoyed with her for getting in so late. She had made Jude get up and answer the door and going back to bed again wasn't going to be a possibility. If she didn't go with Emma, she'd get nagged at to go to church and if she didn't do that she'd be left with her father's frosty silence and newspaper-rattling.

"OK. I'll just put some clothes on. I'll be with you in a minute."

It felt good to be out. The air was cold but the sun was warm. Emma led Jude past gardens bright with blossom and the splashed colour of early spring flowers, to the narrow street that was just called Back Lane. They followed it, behind the church and round the new housing development, to where it skirted the base of the hill.

Jude thought they would go up to the stile and neat signpost which marked the public right of way, but Emma stopped almost immediately. She turned back, took some photographs and then struck out to the right. Jude followed her, struggling through a narrow gap in the overgrown hedge, and found herself surrounded by tall trees at the beginning of a grassy track she didn't even know existed.

"Where does this go?" Jude asked.

"You'll see," Emma replied enigmatically.

The woods were very quiet. All they could hear was the swish of grass and the breaking of twigs under their feet and the occasional whirring chuck of a pheasant.

"I bet you're glad you came now," Emma said after a while. "Lovely here, isn't it?"

Jude looked around. The buds were just breaking and greens of every possible shade, from deep gold to bright jade, misted above her. It was like being underwater. Bluebells stretched away under the trees, their colour just showing through tightly-packed buds.

"Yes, it is," she replied. "On a morning like this, it's difficult to imagine that anything bad could happen here or that it has such a sinister reputation."

"Not like on dark winter nights when, so they do tell, the Horned One rides out with his hounds of hell, and the legions of the numberless dead sweep up all living souls who stray into their path as they follow along behind him!"

"Shut up, Emma." Jude shivered slightly, despite herself. "I was just getting to like the place. I'm sure you make up half those stories."

"No, I don't!" Emma replied indignantly, and then she grinned, "Well, maybe I do – a little bit."

They came round the corner, still laughing and arguing, when Jude suddenly stopped and grabbed Emma's arm, pulling her back. The path led into the open space right behind the Wyatts' cottage.

"What's wrong now?" Emma laughed. "Seen a ghost?"

"Almost. That's Wyatt's car. He must be there. What if he sees us or something?"

"So what if he does?" Emma stepped out in full view of the house. "We're taking a Sunday morning walk on the hill. What's it got to do with him? This is a public right of way, as far as I understand, and this is a free country."

"I don't know . . . it doesn't feel right. What if he thinks we're spying?"

"I don't give a damn what he thinks."

Emma walked out into the clearing behind the cottages and focused her camera. She took a couple of shots and then moved further round to take some more, ending up leaning right over the fence at the end of the gardens.

"There we are," she said as she came back. "Got what I came for."

"What was that?" Jude asked.

"Like I said, you know, the other night. Eileen Stanley put the Wyatts on the map, right? So now I've got the pictures to go with her story."

David Wyatt stayed crouched down inside the house until he was sure they had gone. Seeing Emma Tasker standing there, bold as brass, taking photographs, had given him a real shock. Especially since he'd just been thinking about her. It was almost telepathic. It also confirmed his suspicions of last night. It wasn't paranoia after all. She was on to something, or thought she was, and this just went to prove it. She wasn't alone either. There had been someone with her, keeping out of sight. Jude Hughes. He'd caught a glimpse of golden hair, bright and exotic, in the drab brown-olive colours of the undergrowth.

Perhaps she'd seen him last night, seen him lurking about, and had come back to confirm that he'd been here. He sat on the floor, back against the wall, gnawing at his thumbnail until the skin was ragged. What were they doing? What did they know? He had to find out. He stood up slowly. His hangover was receding now, thank God. What he needed was a hair of the dog. He checked his watch. A couple of places would be open now, Sunday or no Sunday.

"You want me to do what? You have got to be kidding!"

"No, Jude, I'm not." Emma leant forward, her face patient and composed. "I'm deadly serious. You've got to get the beads back off Wyatt. It's the only way we can be absolutely certain."

"And how exactly am I going to do that?"

Emma shrugged. "It shouldn't be that difficult – tell him you want to check the catch or something. Say it's faulty, that the other ones you got from the same batch have all broken."

Simple as that.

Jude did not reply. What was the point? Emma had it all worked out. She stared down at the flat country spread out before them. They had climbed the hill to the very top. The woods clung like a mantle to the lower slopes, but the summit was bare of trees and studded with out-cropping rock. The two girls were sitting in a sheltering nook. There was always a tugging wind up here, even on

117

the hottest days, and although it was still sunny, it was by no means warm, especially when you stopped moving.

The view was spectacular. On a very clear day you could see as far as the Malverns, some even said Wales; but even as they spoke, a dark bank of cloud was obscuring the hills to the west and a sequence of smaller ones were racing their shadows across the lattice of fields towards them. There was a tradition that the weather was never the same on the hill as in other places. Jude shivered. Unlike all the other stories, she knew this one to be true. It could be fine up here and raining everywhere else, or vice versa.

"How do you know they are the same beads?" she asked eventually, hugging her knees. "And even if they are – it doesn't really prove anything."

She watched the scudding clouds and the thin blowing veils of rain falling from them. The thought of approaching Mr Wyatt and trying to retrieve the necklace she had sold to him made her cringe, but she had other doubts about this scheme. Emma could be impetuous and headstrong as well as single-minded. She didn't always think things through before pitching in and it made Jude afraid for her.

"And, anyway, how do you know you can trust this Simon guy? It all sounds a bit sudden to me. I mean, you've only just met him."

"That is completely irrelevant," Emma retorted. "God, Jude! Sometimes you sound like somebody's mother! He wants to find out what happened to his sister and . . ."

"That's another thing. Don't you think it's weird? Him being there, working in the library, and just happening to be her brother?"

"I told you about that. The fact that we're both interested in the same thing is just coincidence."

"A pretty fantastic coincidence!"

Emma shrugged. "Well, that's all it is – fantastic or not. I don't understand why you're getting so upset about it."

"Why didn't you tell me? If I'd been you, I'd have said something first chance I got."

"You aren't me," Emma said, plucking a tuft of grass and letting the wind blow it from her fingers. "We're different, Jude. How many times do I have to tell you? Quite apart from that, this is the first real chance I've had to talk to you about it."

"There was last night."

"Oh, like when? In the car, I suppose, with my mum listening. And as soon as we got there, where were you? Draped around Ben for the rest of the night. I didn't get the feeling that a tap on the shoulder, and 'excuse me, there's something I forgot to tell you, Jude', would have exactly been welcome."

"How about before we went?"

"I was concentrating all my efforts into getting you there, if you recall . . ."

"Oh, OK," Jude conceded, "I just think you should be careful. I worry about you, that's all . . ."

"Well, don't. I can look after myself. If I help him, he'll help me – that's what matters."

"Help you to do what?"

"Find out what really happened to Jenny Beresford. If – *if*," she leant towards Jude, gesturing fiercely, her large dark eyes shining with excitement, "we can prove the beads you found are the very same ones, don't you see how significant that would be? It would be new evidence leading directly to solving the case. It could be huge!

You've got to get those beads for me, Jude. You've just got to!"

Jude stood and walked to the edge of the hilltop, hugging her coat to her. She threw her head back and let the wind blow through her hair. There were other sides to this but Emma just would not see it. She was messing with something they didn't understand, and was completely failing to take into account possible consequences. New evidence could be dangerous. It could lead directly to the killer, and now she was involving someone they hardly knew . . .

On the other hand, Emma was usually pretty astute when it came to judging people, and she seemed to like and trust this Simon. Also it had all happened so long ago. What had Mrs Stanley said? Those involved are dead and gone. Emma was her friend and had appealed for her help. Jude caught at the hair blowing across her face, maybe she was being too cautious. It was getting difficult to keep any sense of proportion.

"We'd better get going. It'll be raining in a minute," she remarked as she returned. Emma took the offered hand and pulled herself up. Jude held on to her for a moment. "I'm not promising anything," she said, the wind snatching at her words. "All I'm saying is, I'll think about it."

Chapter 20

Officially, Jude was working and not to be disturbed, but so far she'd done nothing, apart from lying on the bed staring at the ceiling. Her homework was still piled up on the desk where she'd left it on Friday. The day was slipping away towards evening, it would be dark soon, but she did not put the light on. She folded her hands behind her head and wondered about Emma and her date with Simon.

He was taking her to one of those giant multiscreen places. Emma had phoned earlier, suggesting Jude and Ben make it a foursome. Jude smiled to herself. Perhaps she was bottling out of being alone with him, or maybe she was afraid of being bored. Jude had to decline the invitation, whatever the reason for it. She had not been grounded, not exactly, but she knew that, after last night, going to the pictures on a double date with Emma would not be the most diplomatic thing to do.

Her parents weren't angry any more. It was anxiety more than anger she had stumbled into at one o'clock in the morning, but that made it harder to deal with somehow. She could see the reasons for their protectiveness, feel it. An only child, the inevitable focus of all their love and affection, she sometimes wished she had a couple of naughty younger brothers, like Emma, to deflect some of this attention. Her parents were older too, older than Emma's, and they seemed to worry more, to take everything more seriously. It was as though they wanted to keep her in a box, away from harm, and do all the growing-up for her.

There was something else. It was not Ben himself, they both seemed to like him, or the fact that she was going out with him. She'd had boyfriends before, but they sensed (or her mother did) that this was different. Jude lacked Emma's skill when it came to disguising her emotions. She had not mastered the shuttered gaze and impassive look. Her mother could read her like a book.

It was all unspoken. There had been nothing like a confrontation. Her mother would never ask outright, but if she did, Jude knew how she would have to answer. They had to understand. However much they loved her, she could no longer allow her parents to dictate what she should feel or how she should behave. She could not go on letting them decide what was best for her.

Story of her life – other people always imposed their endings on her. Time to stop all that, she thought, swinging her legs off the bed and sitting up. Time to change.

The wall opposite was still a mess from where she'd torn away the display. That was another example. Originally, it had been her idea, and she'd done most of the background research. Then Emma had taken over.

She put on the desk light, looking for a craft knife, and then set to work, trimming small tears, removing the bits of Sellotape and scraps of paper. There was emulsion downstairs somewhere. She might as well do it properly, paint it over.

Dove grey. Not a shade I would have particularly chosen, she thought as she levered the tin open, but it was all she could find and would have to do. Sometimes it was good to do something mechanical that engaged

122

only the mind's surface. Her thinking on a couple of things began to clear, as marks and blemishes disappeared under an even layer of pastel coating.

First, there was the matter of the beads. If she got them back, it would be because she wanted to, not because of pressure from Emma. She had found them in Ben's shop and she had made them into something. They were hers. Mr Wyatt could have his money back. He couldn't keep them, whatever his reason.

Then there was Ben. Last night in his car, in the silence of the big wood, they'd both tried to tell each other how they felt. They had stumbled about, unable to find the right things to say. All the words you were supposed to use sounded odd when spoken out loud and felt clumsy in the mouth. Then he'd put his arms round her. There had been very little talking after that.

Where did they go from here? Jude wasn't sure, she'd never been in this situation before, but one thing she knew. Whatever happened, whatever they decided to do, would be because she wanted it, not because he wanted her to.

Her mum was calling her from downstairs, the Channel 4 film was about to start and did she want a cup of coffee? Jude collected the brushes and emulsion tray. The smell of new paint filled the room. She opened the window wider, wondering if it would always remind her of how she felt right now, right this minute.

"There a film starting on the other side," Elizabeth Wyatt said, looking up from the TV and radio guide.

But David didn't react, didn't even seem to hear. He appeared totally absorbed by a comedy show. She didn't

123

mind, in fact, she was quite enjoying the host chattering on, and even joined in once or twice with the odd machine-gun bursts of manufactured laughter. But a couple of months ago he would have called this rubbish, would never have dreamt of watching.

He always kept the remote control on the arm of his chair. He had it now, one hand caged protectively over it. The other was pulling at the fringing on the suite. She wished he wouldn't do that. He'd plucked it as bald as a chicken. Good thing it was only the loose sleeve, positioned to prevent wear to the tobacco-coloured Dralon underneath.

David was becoming a worry. She finished a row and flicked over the counter at the end of her knitting needle. He had always been fairly quiet, never talked that much, but how he had really pulled up the drawbridge. The silences could last for days unless she forced him to speak.

At first, she'd put it all down to the death of his mother. They had been so close, emotionally David had never left home, and she had absolutely doted on him. But Elizabeth had a feeling it went deeper than that. Something else was at the bottom of this; his mother's death had just let it out, acted as a catalyst. The counter clicked again as she finished another row. He needed help. He really did. Not that he'd take any notice of her. And their GP was about as useful as a chocolate teapot. His response was, "Time heals all. Things will improve as time goes on. In the meantime – take some of these."

David had not improved as time went on. His behaviour was getting more bizarre by the week. Even that idiot of a doctor seemed to have realized. Some of the stuff he'd got on prescription lately was given to people in loony bins; she'd looked up the computerized

124

labels. Drugs strong enough to knock out donkeys. They only gave things like that to people who were a danger to themselves – or to others.

He needed help which it was beyond her power to give. She was almost at the end of her tether. She would have to get in touch with Alison. Ask her advice, at least. He'd always been fond of Ali, almost like a father to her, Dad Wyatt not being much good in that department by all accounts; but there was no guarantee that David would talk, even to her, about whatever it was eating away at him. Lately, even that relationship seemed to have curdled. He used his poisoned wheedling sarcasm now whenever they were together. Elizabeth's mouth set in a grim line as she counted stitches. He could turn words into thin little knives. He was good at that, very good indeed. At the moment, even the mention of Ali's name was enough to spark a stream of bitter, barbed remarks.

The picture on the TV changed. The titles and opening shots were playing in twin miniature on her husband's glasses. She looked over at him, suddenly chilled by the feeling that there was no one home behind those lenses. No one she recognized as her husband, that is.

Chapter 21

"Wonderful," Emma mumbled into the phone, through a mouthful of toast. "Great film – absolute buckets of popcorn . . ."

Jude laughed. "Who could ask for more on a first date?"

"And that's not all. But," Emma's voice became clearer as she swallowed the last of her toast, "you'll have to wait for the rest. I'm not going in yet."

"Why not?"

"Something I want to do first."

"What shall I tell Marlow?"

"Tell him I've got cripplingly bad period pains. That should stop him enquiring further. I'll be in lunch-time-ish."

Jude laughed again. Mr Marlow, their tutor, looked so young he was always being mistaken for a sixth-former, and he had that sort of pink-and-white skin that registered the slightest blush.

"Got to go now." Emma glanced out of the window. Mrs Stanley's small white Fiat was turning into the yard outside. "See you later."

"OK. See you, then."

Emma put down the phone and ran lightly up the stairs, back to her bedroom. Mrs Stanley was the reason she was staying at home but she didn't want to see her, not just yet.

She lay on the bed, flicking through *Elle*. There was

plenty to tell Jude. Last night had gone well. He had brought the photograph with him. It was on her desk now. A good-quality print. Being hidden away from the light all those years had kept the colours as bright as the day it was taken. Should enlarge, no problem. Even as it was, the beads showed quite clearly. She'd been over the whole thing with a magnifying glass.

Simon had been a bit reluctant to hand it over but she'd convinced him to trust her and had promised to be careful with it. He still did not take her entirely seriously. Although he wasn't really all that much older, he had a tendency to treat her like a kid. He was considerate and entertaining but there was a distance, wariness even, behind his surface charm which she found puzzling. It was refreshing to go to the cinema with someone who actually wanted to watch the film – the last boy she'd been with had swarmed all over her the minute the lights went down – but afterwards, when he took her home, she'd been expecting slightly more than a brotherly kiss.

She got up and went quietly to the bedroom door, opening it a fraction to stand and listen. The old farmhouse was big and rambling but it was surprising how sound travelled. The clattering of dishes had finished in the kitchen and the dish-washer was getting into its cycle. It was time to move. Emma glided silently along the landing as the droning of the Hoover threaded in and out of the downstairs rooms.

"I'm sorry," Emma said, with a mock apologetic smile. "Did I startle you?"

"You know bloody well you did!" Mrs Stanley's voice was loud with shock. She pulled the vacuum cleaner out from where she'd jammed it under a table and her hand was shaking as she fumbled with the switch to turn it off.

"Creeping up on people like that. Could have given me a heart attack."

She turned round to face Emma.

"What are you doing home from school?"

"Not feeling too well. I came down to make a coffee. Thought you might like a cup."

"All right." Mrs Stanley parked the Hoover neatly and followed Emma into the kitchen. "I need something to get over the shock."

"What's the matter?" she asked when they were seated at the kitchen table.

"Oh, you know . . ." Emma said, trying to look suitably bashful and letting the words trail off.

"Monthlies?"

Emma nodded.

Mrs Stanley clucked sympathetically. Next to people dying, gynaecology and menstruation were her favourite topics. Among the women of the village she was an acknowledged expert on such matters.

"Like my Susan. She's a martyr to it. I was and all, before my operation . . ."

"It's not too bad now," Emma said quickly, in order to head off a major surgical description. "I'll be going in later."

"How's your research?" Mrs Stanley asked, after a moment or two, giving the third word a slight ironic stress.

"Oh, OK." Emma shrugged, then added, "Not so well actually."

"Told you, didn't I?"

Eileen Stanley gave her a knowing, irritating look as she reached in her apron pocket for her cigarettes.

"Want one?" she asked, offering the packet.

"Umm, yes. OK."

Emma accepted a cigarette and leant towards the flame of the proffered lighter. Mrs Stanley enjoyed little acts of subversion like that and Emma was quite willing to go along with it in order to gain her confidence.

"After all these years – folk still don't want to talk about it. That's the difficulty."

Emma nodded her agreement. "Even when they do," she said, exhaling smoke, "it's the same old story. No new evidence. That's the problem. So far, no one's told me anything I didn't already know about this."

"I did." Mrs Stanley studied the glowing coal on the end of her cigarette.

"Yes. You did," Emma conceded. "You've been the only one, though. I was wondering ... would you be prepared to help me some more?"

Mrs Stanley did not reply immediately. Her pencilled eyebrows drew together in a frown as she made up her mind, puckering the thick foundation on her forehead.

Emma watched, tense. She had worked out her strategy carefully. It centred round flattering the older woman's unrivalled local knowledge, but also, and this would be far more difficult, manipulating the most manipulative person Emma had ever met – rivalling her in deviousness.

"Depends," Mrs Stanley said eventually, "on what you want to know."

"Well, first off, can you tell me who the children are in this photograph? It was taken at the fête – the day Jenny disappeared."

Mrs Stanley scanned the print Emma put before her on the table.

"That's easy. The one in the middle is Jenny Beresford. The other two, let me see ..." she picked up the photo and held it nearer for closer scrutiny. "The little one is

129

Clare Conrad and the bigger one is Alison Wyatt. Never seen this before." She turned it over to examine the back. "Where did you get it?"

Emma ignored the last question. She did not feel like discussing Simon with anyone, let alone Eileen Stanley.

"What were the Wyatts like?" she asked instead.

"What do you mean?"

"You know, as a family. In particular, can you tell me anything about the other brother, Robbie?"

"Robbie Wyatt." Mrs Stanley shook her head. "He was a tearaway-and-a-half, he was. Nothing nasty, mind, but always up to something, always in trouble. Very different from their David – he was the quiet one. Not very, you know, outgoing. Even when David was quite old you'd see him hanging around, playing with much younger kiddies. David was the oldest by a couple of years but Robbie always seemed to be looking after him."

Mrs Stanley paused. That photograph had been taken after the fancy-dress competition; maybe an hour, less than an hour, before the disturbance in the Wyatts' garden. She heard again the boys' voices, losing their new-found masculinity, breaking back to childhood, and then Ma Wyatt adding her voice to theirs, deep and carrying in its urgency, trying to find out what was the matter, trying to calm them down. The panic and intensity had drawn her and kept her standing at the window, half naked. Something about what was going on between them, and her paralysing fear of Mrs Wyatt, had caught her in the moment until it had become fixed in her mind, frozen like a tableau. She shrugged and shook her head.

"I can tell you something else about the Wyatts – and this is true as God is my witness – if you still want to know."

"Yes. Anything. I want to know."

Mrs Stanley lit another cigarette.

"That night," she pointed to Jenny in the photograph, "the night of the day she disappeared, I had to go down to the village. The old man's leg was playing up and he wanted me to go to the pub and get him a flagon of cider. They kept a barrel behind the bar in them days, and they'd fill you a flagon to take home. It was a proper village pub then, not like it is now with all them fancy beers and chalked-up pricey menus. Anyway, he kept nagging me and I kept ignoring him, hoping he'd forget. Finally he starts shouting, and he had a terrible temper on him, so off I went – down the old track, back of the hill. Do you know it?"

"Yes," Emma said impatiently, crushing out her cigarette. "I went up that way yesterday. I know it."

"I was on my way back. It was past closing-time, I'd stayed for a bit of a chat, but it was still hot out, very close, and that dark – you couldn't see your hand. Felt like the clouds were pressing right down. There was lightning flickering on the hills all about, and every now and then you could hear thunder, distant like, growling around. I was really hurrying, trying to get back without a drenching, and you know the hill – there are that many stories about it and – I've lived there all my life – but on a night like that you can really believe them. I was thinking about black dogs and headless ladies when I damn near pitched right into them. Gave me a real fright, I can tell you."

"Who did?"

"The Wyatts, David and Robbie. They were as surprised as me – David was that pale, looked like a ghost himself, but their Robbie was different. Quick as a flash, he starts acting the fool, singing 'Goodnight Eileen, good-

131

night Eileen, I'll see you in my dreams'. Should have been, 'Goodnight Irene', but he always changed it."

"So?" Emma had followed all this as closely as she could but, so far, had failed to pick up the significance.

"So, this." Mrs Stanley nudged a column of ash off her cigarette and her blue eyes narrowed, becoming shrewd and hard.

"Next morning Ma Wyatt comes into the garden while I'm pegging clothes out, and starts to chat. She asks me about the day before, what had happened, like she'd missed it all. Then she shakes her head and asks:

" 'Any sign of her?'

"I said, 'Not as far as I know. They're carrying on searching today.'

"She says she'll be sending David and Robbie down to lend a hand. Then she says:

" 'I had a big job on yesterday, over Morton way. Had to take my lads to help me with it. Good for nothing when they got in. Just sat there all night watching the telly.'

"She finishes pegging out her line and in she goes." Mrs Stanley stubbed her cigarette in the saucer she was using for an ashtray. "She never spoke to me again about it, but that was her story and she stuck by it."

"But you knew it wasn't true!" Emma exclaimed. "That was vital information, Eileen. You should have told someone!"

Eileen Stanley shrugged her ample shoulders. "I owed her. She knew I wouldn't say a word. She'd helped me out of a bit of trouble."

"What kind of trouble?"

Eileen Stanley gave Emma a measuring look. The question sounded genuine enough, but the girl was clever.

She'd got Eileen to tell her something she'd never told a living soul. It was hard to tell now if she was playing the innocent.

"What kind of trouble do you think? What kind of trouble do girls usually get into?"

Emma blushed to the roots of her hair. Mrs Stanley chuckled at the girl's discomfort.

"It wasn't like now, you know. Quick trip into hospital on the National Health and all over. It was all private clinics in them days – cost a fortune – unless you knew someone. In this village that was Ma Wyatt. She'd give you something to do the trick."

"How?"

"She knew things – got it off her mother, and her mother, going way back. They were the ones called in when a baby was due – or somebody died. They all have their babies in the hospital now. But old Ma Wyatt was still called in to lay people out. Remember old Mr Roper . . ."

"Knew things? What sort of things?" Emma cut in. "You mean – like witchcraft?" She leant forward. "Eileen, you don't think the things they said at the time, about the murder, could be true, do you? The way she was killed, the marks on her face . . ."

"Witchcraft! Don't be daft!" Eileen Stanley's pealing laugh broke off suddenly and she listened. "Sounds like your mum," she said briskly, scooping up the ashtray and dumping the cups in the sink. "You'd better get back upstairs if you're supposed to be poorly."

Emma stood up.

"Forget the witchcraft. That was all rubbish, made up by outsiders; people who didn't know the village," Mrs Stanley added without looking round from Dettoling the

133

surfaces. "Take the Wyatts, they were close, a close-knit family. They had their version of what they was doing that day, police weren't going to shake 'em on it. And if other folk knew different, they probably had reason to keep quiet – like me. Old Ma Wyatt knew things about me and I owed her. You've got to understand, it's not the same now. Take your parents – if you'd been with a lad and got into trouble, they wouldn't be too happy about it but they'd help you. I'd be the same with my girls. But back then? I'm speaking God's honest truth when I tell you, Emma, my dad would have killed me if he'd found out."

Mrs Tasker struggled in with her shopping and put it on the counter. There was no sign of Emma, and Eileen Stanley had gone back to her hoovering, but the two coffee cups and the faint smell of cigarette smoke told their own story.

The kettle was still warm; they'd probably been gossiping all the time she was out. It was not something Marion Tasker felt entirely happy about. What had Emma called her? An excellent source of information. Eileen Stanley was certainly that. A finger in every pie? More like both fists up to the elbow.

She spooned coffee into a mug and clicked the kettle back on. Marion herself tried never to get involved in the intrigues and politics that fuelled the life of the village. It always led to trouble – mostly petty squabbling, but sometimes it burned deep and turned into feuding that went on for years. Certain families had not been speaking to each other for the best part of a century. It was usually over land and property but quarrels were passed on like

134

precious heirlooms. Eileen Stanley was busy stoking one at the moment about who owned the rough paddock at the back of her mother's cottage. She had received a letter from David Wyatt's solicitor just the other week and was still steaming about it.

Marion sipped her coffee and gazed out of the kitchen window at the slightly undulating ground leading up to Mitre Hill. It still carried the pattern of the medieval field system. The Wyatts and Stanleys had probably been at it hammer and tongs way back then. She did not know exactly what Eileen Stanley was up to now but she certainly did not want Emma involved in it.

"Hello, love. How are you feeling? I've brought you a drink."

Mrs Tasker came over to the desk where Emma was working and laid the mug down where she could find a space.

"What are you doing?" she asked, resting an arm lightly across her daughter's shoulders, and then laughed. "You were at death's door this morning. If you're working you must be feeling better. What's this?"

Emma, trying to get everything Eileen Stanley had told her down on paper as quickly as possible before she forgot it, was a fraction too late with the covering hand. Her mother had picked up the photograph.

"Let's have a look." She turned the picture slightly, seeking to look at the three children grouped in the foreground. The hand on Emma's shoulder tightened as she recognized then. "Clare didn't give you this, did she? Where did you get it? I'm not at all sure I like this stuff you're getting into . . ."

"It's just research, Mum." Emma shrugged the hand off her shoulder, resenting the interference, wanting to get on with it. "For that article I'm doing. I'm not 'getting into' anything."

"OK. So where did this come from?"

Emma stared at her desk, rearranging the pens and fiddling with the Tipp-Ex.

"A friend. A friend gave it to me," she said eventually.

"Which friend, exactly? Jude?"

"No. Someone else."

"Who?"

"Simon. You know, from the library. The guy I went out with last night."

"Where did he get it?"

"He found it. Among some papers. He knew I was interested so he let me have it. That's all. It's no big deal. I've nearly finished, anyway. I've only got a bit more to do on it." Emma didn't like lying, but the truth was bound to freak her mother out. "So can I have it back now, please?" She held her hand up to receive the photograph. "Mum?"

It floated down on to the table. Mrs Tasker was reluctant to let it go and wanted to ask more – about this young man from the library for one thing – but she was torn. Emma wasn't a child to be interrogated and prevented from doing this or that for her own safety. Parts of her life were no longer for public display. Marion Tasker respected that. Her daughter was a young woman now, with adult tastes and views, and if she judged that this was a serious endeavour, it must be treated that way.

Still, this whole Jenny Beresford business made her uneasy. It had done from the start if she were really honest with herself. Clare had sought to reassure her, put it in perspective. It was historical research, she had said, (as though that made it all OK) an academic exercise. But it had nagged at Marion, almost to the point where she wanted to stop Emma from continuing with it.

Coombe Ashleigh was like the village pond. It appeared nice and clear but if you stirred deep enough, God knows what might surface. What if they found something no one else had yet discovered? What if they had already done so?

It was certainly possible. Marion did not underestimate Emma's intelligence and knew that once she set her mind on something she would pursue it with ruthless persistence. She held the door half open and turned to look at her daughter. This was getting to be more than just some project. There was a kind of suppressed excitement about her, the way she was sitting there, tense in her chair. She was getting as obsessed as poor old Jack Russell. Couldn't wait to be alone to gloat over all this stuff she'd collected.

That photograph. Emma was going over it now with a magnifying glass. Just seeing it had made Marion feel strange. It was eerie. The print was as fresh as if it had been taken recently, but two of the children were grown women and the other was dead.

She could remember them posing for it. Jenny had won the fancy-dress competition, the other two had been runners-up. She could see them now, jostling each other, giggling with excitement, full of the importance that winning gave them. She'd watched from her station behind the Girl Guides' tombola, slightly resentful that she was too old to be in it any more, thinking Ali should have won. She looked dashing and wicked, every inch a pirate, while Jenny made a very dumpy little flapper and half the things she had on didn't go together, but Mrs Harrison was the head of the judging committee. They were standing in front of the marquee. You could even see the guy ropes if you looked carefully.

She remembered everything. The photograph brought it all back. It was one of those days that starts just like any other, and then some momentous event occurs to act like acid and etch it on to the memory, clearer than yesterday.

The period after the body was discovered remained, in Marion's mind, the most disturbing time. It brought out the worst aspects of the village. Little more than a child, she'd been old enough to hear and understand the whispers, the distrust, the rumours flying around. People seemed intent on pointing the finger at anyone who came from outside, making up preposterous tales. Even Anna Beresford had not been exempt. Some had even tried to implicate her in the death of her own child, hinting at a darkness in her past, known only to Harrison, her solicitor. He had taken pity on her, given her a job, they said, but anyone could see she wasn't right in the head, a few pence short of a shilling.

Things bad begun . . .

The tag of a quote tolled like a bell inside her head. She closed the door. It was time to confront her daughter.

"Emma," she said with quiet authority, "I really don't want you to go on with this."

Chapter 22

"Hi," Ben jogged up the corridor and then measured his stride to hers, falling into step beside her, "Emma shown up?"

"No." Jude shook her head. "She said she was coming in but I don't know where she is."

"How about Wyatt? Did you find him?"

"Drawn a blank there too." Jude grinned. "Mr Talbot said I was wasting my time looking in the staffroom. Said I'd be better trying the bar in the Feathers, or failing that the Queen's Head."

"Not doing too well, are you?"

"Not brilliantly. No."

"Come here," he slipped his arm round her waist and pulled her to him.

"Ben! What are you doing? Someone might see us . . ."

Jude leant against the wall, breathless, laughing. She had not thought it was possible to be this happy. What if anybody saw? People would think they were crazy. It would be most uncool to be caught snogging in the corridor like a couple of kids.

"Are you ready to go home, then?" Ben took a thick strand of golden hair and arranged it carefully behind her ear. "Or shall we find a nice empty classroom . . ."

"No. Things to do." Jude was trying to sound brisk and efficient, even though the way he was looking at her made her feel something entirely different. "Come on," she

139

linked her arm into his, pulling him along. "You can help me."

"Where to?" Ben said as he turned the ignition. "Have you got the address?"

"Well, not exactly," Jude bit her lip. "I thought you might know. I mean, you are in his tutor group."

"So what? Doesn't mean I know where he lives." He leant back and folded his arms, letting the engine idle. "Wyatt's not exactly the matey type, is he? He doesn't go in for little get-togethers and barbecues like Clare Conrad and her mates. Look it up in the telephone book."

"I did. He's ex-directory. Oh, well," Jude sighed, "it doesn't really matter. I can tell Emma I tried, at least."

Ben put the car into gear.

"Don't need to give up yet," he said, looking over his shoulder as he reversed into the emptying car park. "I've got an idea."

"I can't!" Jude whispered ferociously, eyeing the fair head bent over the computer console. "I hardly know him!"

"Yes, you do. You were talking to him Saturday night, we both were. He's your best friend's boyfriend for Chrissake!"

"I don't think he's her boyfriend, not exactly . . ."

"Doesn't matter a whole lot what he is." He pushed her gently in the back and moved towards the CD racks. "Get over there and do the business!"

"Hello. How may I help you? Oh, hello there . . ." His voice changed from bright professional enquiry to genuine friendliness. "It's Jude, isn't it?" He was already looking through her, trying to see behind her. "Is Emma with you?"

"No, she hasn't been in school today. Off sick."

"Oh." His mouth turned down with disappointment. "Nothing serious, I hope?"

Jude smiled. "Nothing exactly life-threatening. She should be in tomorrow . . ."

"In? Here? At the library?"

"No. I meant school, actually."

He saw by her eyes that Jude had caught his fleeting look of disappointment.

"She had something for me," he said, by the way of explanation. "I rather thought . . . Anyway," he leant back in his chair and folded his arms. "What can I do for you, then?"

"I wanted to ask you a favour," she said, unfolding a piece of paper.

He listened as Jude outlined her request and then studied the name on the note.

"What you're asking is against library rules, strictly not allowed. But seeing you're a friend of Emma's . . ." He pulled the chair towards the computer and started keying in codes and letters. "Don't tell anyone, though. They could have my job for this. And . . . bingo!" He looked at the screen in front of him. "Borrows a lot. History mostly. Sound like him?"

"That's the one." Jude grinned at him over the desk.

"Do you want the phone too?" he asked as he wrote. "Well, here you are," he jotted the number under the address and tore the sheet off the scratch pad in front of him. "Might as well have it all."

She left with the tall dark guy she'd been with at the party. Must be her boyfriend. What was his name? Ben something. He watched them leave and then reached for the phone by the side of his computer station.

"Can you get the phone, Emma? My hands are wet."

"Hello . . ."

"Hi! It's me. How are you feeling?"

"Oh, hi," Emma said. She turned her back when she recognized Simon's voice but with her mother at the sink and a tableful of little brothers, it was going to be hard to keep this call private. "I'm OK. How did you know I was ill, anyway?"

"I've just seen your friend, Jude. She told me."

"Oh. Where?"

"In the library. That's where I am now, wasting rate-payers' money. When can I see you? Tonight?"

"I'm afraid that's not possible . . ."

"Why not? You said . . ."

"I know. Can't be helped. Sorry."

"When then? Tomorrow?"

"Tomorrow's fine, any particular time?"

"Can't you talk?"

Emma swung round. Her mother was peeling potatoes but you could tell by the way she stood that she was listening out for every word said. Her brothers and their friend were sitting in a row like Huey, Lewy and Dewy, crunching cornflakes. They couldn't even be quiet when they were eating.

"No. Not easily."

"Right. When? Lunch-time? After school?"

"After school would be better."

"OK. If that's the best you can do. See you then."

"Yes. I'll look forward to it."

"Who was that?" her mother asked as soon as she hung up the phone.

"Assistant Editor at the *Advertiser*," Emma replied nonchalantly. "Wants me to go in to see him tomorrow, thinks he might have some work for me. I want to get some stuff together to show him. Give me a shout when tea's ready."

Emma loaded a game into her computer; she hadn't played one for ages but she didn't feel like doing anything else, just wanted to get into something completely mindless. After twenty minutes she was raking her fingers through her short dark hair in a rage of frustration. She yanked the disk out and tossed it away. Huey, Lewy or Dewy would have got more than that, it was her lowest score ever.

Not scoring high in any department at the moment. She stood up and paced around, arms folded across her chest, wondering what to do. She had listened patiently this morning, keeping her face quite impassive, as her mother had stated, as reasonably as possible, her worries and fears about the research Emma was doing and why she should not go on with it. They had both tried hard not to let it escalate into a full-scale row. They didn't fight very much but when they did, they tended to really hurt each other.

She could see her mother's point of view. Maybe it was right to leave the Beresford case alone now, not do any more about it, find another article for the journalism competition. But she could not. She had snapped shut her folder with a "That's that" air of theatrical finality and no intention of keeping her word. She fully intended to carry on, in secret. Not just for herself, but for Simon, or rather for his mother.

He had told Emma more about her last night. The torment she had suffered over the years and how it had affected him. How she had ignored the love of her real live surviving child, to grieve after little Jenny, eaten up with guilt. Finding out exactly what had happened might help her, allow her to forgive herself.

Despite what other people thought, Emma was not really cynical. A happy child from a loving home, she had not realized how privileged she was until she listened to Simon's life of neglect and emptiness. Something about his intensity still rather frightened her, but he had touched her, and she had given her word to help him. Emma did not want to break that promise, even if it meant lying to her own mother about it.

Chapter 23

The next morning David Wyatt stood in the bathroom, in his vest, pyjama bottoms loosely knotted around his skinny hips, peering into the mirror. Funny, he always shaved with his glasses off and always went through this ritual facial examination before he started.

He leant nearer, into his reflection. His hair, still wet from the shower, lay against his skull in thin strands of dark auburn. God, he grimaced, he was getting to look just like the old man. His hair used to go back, just like that. He could see him now, standing in front of the hall mirror, swiping at the sides with those twin brushes he had, before he went down the pub. Robbie used to wait until he'd gone out and then pinch some of his Brylcreem. For a second, at the thought of his brother, a fleeting smile softened the face he was scrutinizing.

His old man. David massaged his neck, not as scraggy as his yet. He'd been a devil for the drink though, didn't know what he was doing half the time. He didn't want to go the same way as his father in that respect. He stared into his own bloodshot blue eyes. He ought to ease up on the booze a bit.

He squeezed a blob of shaving foam into his palm and spread it over his cheeks, chin and neck. There wasn't any of this stuff back then. It came in funny little sticks or a solid block, you had to go at it hard with a brush to work up a lather.

He remembered watching his dad at the kitchen sink with his braces down, peering into the little piece of cracked mirror. Then, when he himself had started to shave, Ali had watched him. The same eyes. Looking up into his. He'd dab some of his lather on to her chin and she'd scrape it off with the back of a comb, dipping it into the water, flicking off the foam, copying him. When Robbie told her, "You're a girl. You'll never need to shave," she'd just shrugged and carried on. "He's wrong," she'd whispered after he'd gone, "when I grow up I'll be just like you, David."

He looked up, surprised to find tears spilling down into the white foam on his cheeks. He picked up the yellow-and-white plastic disposable razor. This really was not good enough. He had to get a grip. If he had been using his dad's old cut-throat, he'd have had to grow a beard, his hand was shaking so badly.

Downstairs the front door slammed. She was back from taking the kids to school. Was it that time already?

"David?"

She was hovering at the door but he could tell by the tone of her voice that she was coming in. Christ. He hated it when she did that. Thought she could waltz in whenever she liked, that was the trouble with ensuite bathrooms.

"Yes?"

"Did you go into school yesterday?"

"Of course I did! You saw me off in the morning. Where did you think I was going?"

"I really don't know, David."

She was in now, somewhere behind him, fiddling about with the bath taps.

"What made you ask?"

He swilled the razor to start on the other side of his face. Little tiny red hairs, bright as fusewire, gleamed in the globs of foam dispersing across the surface of the water.

"It's just a girl came here. After school. She'd been looking for you all day and couldn't find you."

His eyes looked away from hers in the mirror as he concentrated on the next area he was preparing to shave.

"Came here?" his voice was distorted as he pulled the skin taut. "What girl? What was her name?"

"Jude Hughes. Something about a string of beads you bought off her for my birthday . . ."

The razor slipped in his hand, the thin edge of blade nicking his skin. He'd cut himself. Shit! Blood welled crimson and spread into the surrounding foam, turning it pinkish.

He picked up a flannel and wiped the mess off his face.

"Pass me some of that bog roll, will you? I've bloody cut myself!" He dabbed at the area, trying to stem the flow with tissue paper. "I don't even teach her. She's one of Clare Conrad's. I haven't the faintest idea what she wanted here. I don't know what she's talking about!"

"Couldn't find him, and his wife completely blanked me out. Obviously didn't have a clue – so embarrassing. Sorry, Emma."

"That's OK. Thanks for trying."

It was lunch-time. Jude and Emma had walked down to the river. The day had started bright but was clouding over now and the wind was coming up, riffling the surface of the water. Blossom from the cherry trees showered down on them as they stood side by side, silent now, leaning on a low wall, staring into the river.

"What are you going to do?" Jude asked eventually.

"I don't know," Emma shrugged, thrusting her hands deeper in her pockets. "Kind of ground to a bit of a halt, hasn't it?"

Jude reached over and brushed away some petals that had caught like confetti in Emma's dark hair.

"Something will turn up, don't worry."

"What if it doesn't?" Emma hunched her shoulders and frowned down at the water. "What am I going to tell Simon? He's going to think I've been winding him up. He's going to think I'm a total idiot!"

Jude laughed. "No he isn't. Why should he? You found out who the other girls were, that's what he asked you to do. What more can he expect?"

Emma didn't answer. She was going through one of her swings from enthusiasm to despair. It was great as long as everything was going fine, but Emma didn't cope too well with reverses. A clock struck the quarter-hour and Jude checked the time on her watch.

"We'd better go," she said, and then added, "There is one more thing we could try . . ."

"What?"

"Ben thought of it. Go down to the shop, check the books. If the beads came from a house clearance, we might find a name that fits. Also Stevie's back and might remember something. He said to ask Stevie about it."

"Hey! What a great idea!" Emma grinned, her face cleared and the sparkle came back into her dark eyes. "I'd hang on to him if I was you, Jude. That boy's a genius! I copied the photo as soon as I got in, so I've got spare prints. Take one with you. See if Stevie recognizes the beads from it."

Chapter 24

Alison Wyatt settled herself by the window in first class. Midweek, midafternoon, the train was not crowded but her bag and coat on the next seat, and papers spread all over the table, were enough to discourage any other travellers from joining her. She sat tense with impatience, waiting to get out of London, wanting to see Clare.

This was the first time she'd gone home since her mother's funeral, and that was the last time she and Clare had met. They had hardly spoken. Alison, overwhelmed by waves of conflicting emotion: guilt, relief, and guilt again, had held herself deliberately aloof. She had to appear hard to keep from breaking apart. And, anyway, what was there to say? Clare had smiled and held her close for a moment to show she understood.

Before that, her infrequent trips home had been occasioned by her mother's worsening health. Each visit charted a stage in her decline. Until the last one. David had called her at work. Their mother was in hospital. She'd had to be taken in.

When Alison arrived, David was fussing round the bed.

"Soon have you home, Mum. Soon have you home . . ."

Perhaps he believed it, but no one else did. One look was enough to tell you; Mrs Wyatt was never going to leave that hospital again. Alison came into the room thinking she was already dead. Only her eyes were alive, black and bright in the wasted face.

What did she feel? What was there to feel? Shovel it into a ditch and cover it over, along with everything else.

Although the sun was no longer shining, Alison reached into her bag for a pair of dark glasses. The long train was beginning its slow slide down the platform and out of the station; negotiating a way, jolting and tentative, across the wide expanses of criss-cross tangled track. Graffiti names and pieces decorated carriages shunted into sidings, concrete cuttings, even the sides of bridges. She'd seen it in New York, but never noticed it here before. Its presence surprised her, making her feel disoriented, as though she was in a foreign country.

She adjusted her sunglasses, flicking her fringe out of her face. Her short red hair fell back immediately into the exact geometric lines of a very expensive cut.

The train gathered speed, sweeping out into suburbia. The driver, or senior conductor or someone, introduced himself with the rapid laconic delivery of an airline pilot. Alison closed her eyes. She always found the outskirts of London, the endless semis with their prominent drain-pipes and boring back gardens, singularly depressing.

The dream began the same. She was in that dark place barred with light. The hot airlessness of the interior, the peculiar smell, the familiar suffocating feeling.

But this time was different. She could see more – things she had never noticed before. The rough brick walls and the beaten earth floor, barrels and sacks scattered about, shelves covered in rusty old tins and dark unlabelled bottles half-full of nameless liquids. She knew where she was. She knew exactly where she was. Even in the dream she had a sense of anticipation, a mixture of fear and

151

excitement. The allotment sheds. The ramshackle remnants of the outhouses belonging to an old farm that had once existed right in the middle of the village.

Over on the far side, under a filthy fly-specked cobwebbed window, was the workbench. Made out of old railway ties, stacked up and lashed together. At one end of it was the big iron vice.

Alison began to move, slowly, quietly. She was not alone in there and had to avoid, at all costs, anything sudden. Her foot slipped, as though she had trodden on small pebbles or pieces of grit. She looked down. Green glass beads sprayed and skittered away from under her sandals.

She froze. Her movement had roused the dark figure, bent over in the corner. Eyes gleamed white as they turned towards Alison silhouetted in the doorway, haloed in light.

Teeth shone as he came and bent down over her. Words came to her in an urgent husky whisper.

"You weren't here, Ali. You never came here. You never saw it. You never heard it. You will never tell anyone. Ever. Ever. Ever in your life. Do you understand what I'm saying to you?"

His hands held her shoulders like steel rods, his fingers gripping at each word, shaking and hurting, biting through flesh to the bone. The eyes staring down, pupils hugely dilated, rimmed with pale blue, were exactly the same shade as her own. The eyes of David, her brother.

Alison nodded to show that she understood and stepped away from him. In the moment it took to cross into the blinding light she had forgotten, taking with her no memory into that June afternoon, no recollection of what had happened in that dark place with its smell of weed-killer, blood and pesticide.

"Sorry to disturb you, Miss." Another hand shook her gently by the shoulder, bringing her back to the present. "Could I see your ticket?"

"Yes, of course." Ali fumbled for her wallet, trying to adjust to her surroundings. "Here."

"That was some dream you were having," he laughed as he clipped the side of it, "muttering away to yourself. I talk in my sleep sometimes, drives the wife crazy. I grind my teeth." He grinned, teeth very white under a grey grizzled moustache. "Here you go."

She looked up to accept her ticket and thank him. His broad black face creased into a wider smile and his dark eyes filled with recognition.

"Wait a minute! Haven't I seen you? I know – on the telly. Alison Wyatt Reporting. Wait till I tell the wife. We're big fans, never miss it. I thought I'd seen you before."

'No, actually I'm not. I just look a bit like her. That's all."

"I'm sorry . . ."

"That's OK." Alison Wyatt shrugged and smiled. "Happens all the time. Don't worry about it."

He waved a hand and continued his affable way down the carriage. Alison turned the window, staring at the racing landscape with unseeing eyes. Images rushed inside her, filling the vacuum of memory. She could do nothing to prevent it. She could no longer hide. A steel door had slammed open inside her mind, exposing what had been hidden all this time.

The train rocked slightly as it reached maximum velocity, returning Alison to the country of her birth, to a childhood mutilated and stained by murder.

Chapter 25

"Jude might be able to get the beads back, but don't hold your breath, so it looks like I was wasting your time. I'm really sorry, Simon." Emma pushed herself away from the café table and folded her arms. "I hope you don't think I've been winding you up."

"Of course not," he shrugged, "you don't need to apologize. Anyway . . ."

A waitress came up to take their order, interrupting him.

"Tea, please. Do you want tea, Emma?"

"Oh, yes. I suppose so . . . Darjeeling. No milk. Lemon."

"Anything else?"

"Umm," Emma examined the menu. "Yes. Chocolate fudge cake."

"Cream or ice-cream?" the waitress asked as she wrote it down.

"Both."

Simon shook his head and smiled. "Just tea for me."

"That's it then," Emma said, shutting the menu and handing it to the waitress.

"So? You can't keep me in suspense any longer," he said as soon as she had gone. "Who are they?"

Emma reached into her school bag. She'd worked hard in the darkroom, enlarging and taking copies, and had then placed the original in a special folder for safekeep-

155

ing. Simon cleared a space as she snapped the fastenings back, extracted the photograph and placed it in front of him. She leaned towards him, her long, slim fingers playing across the figures.

"The little one's Clare . . ." she started to say.

"Who's the Pirate?" he interrupted immediately.

Emma looked up at him in surprise.

"That's Alison. Alison Wyatt. You've probably seen her. She has a programme . . ."

"I know who Alison Wyatt is."

The words came out harder than he'd meant, cutting across hers, and then he was silent for a long time. The waitress came and went with their order but Simon just sat there, staring at the photograph. His hands gripped tighter, crushing the corners, until the print began to shake. It was a girl. The Pirate was a girl! All these years, he'd thought, assumed: in his dreams and fantasy games it had always been a boy. He felt weird, slightly light-headed and sick. All the time it was a girl. Of course. How very stupid!

He put the photograph down on the table and carefully stirred the tea Emma had placed before him. What else had he got wrong about this? So much of his inner life was based on illusion, it felt as though some vast iri-descent bubble had burst inside him. Even now, as an adult, he was still carrying on the same fantasy. Simon the hero. And what task had he set himself to do? To reveal the truth, give his mother peace of mind, after all this time? Depended what the truth was. It might be just as necessary to protect her from it. He realized suddenly that he didn't want to know what had happened to Jenny all those years ago. He hadn't been thinking straight or he would have seen this before. It was best to leave the past alone.

"Simon? What's the matter?"

Emma was staring at him, had been for a while, her dark expressive eyes full of concern.

"Nothing." He frowned and pushed at the floating lemon with his spoon. "I have to go." He wiped his mouth on a napkin and got up quickly, almost overturning the chair. "I'm sorry."

Emma sat for some time after he left, watching the ice-cream melt white goo into the rich black stickiness of her chocolate cake. She tried a couple of mouthfuls but immediately felt sick. For the first time in her life she just wasn't hungry. What was the matter with him? Why had he just left like that? Was it something she'd said? Something she had done? She sighed and drained the last of her tea. Even that was stewed and cold now, an oily residue floating on the top, the delicate lemon overpowered by tannin.

She picked up the five-pound note he'd left on the table and paid the bill.

Outside it was raining. At first Emma didn't mind walking in the rain. It suited her mood. For a moment she toyed with the idea of going to see him in the library, but just as quickly dismissed it. She didn't run after people. Not her style. She recalled part of the 'discussion' she'd had with her mother the previous morning, the part that had been about Simon. Her mother had put on her special tentative, tactful, "I'm not interfering, but . . ." voice and gone on about "older men". Emma had smiled at the time, but maybe she had a point. It certainly didn't seem so funny right now. Neither did the rain. It was soaking through her cardigan, dripping off her fringe and running down the back of her neck. The fine drizzle was turning into a downpour.

Emma rounded the corner at a run, just in time to see the bus pull out with a full load of passengers. She stood there, cursing. There would not be another for an hour and there was no way of stopping this one, short of throwing herself in front of it.

Where could she go? The golden arches of McDonald's beckoned. At least it wasn't raining in there. She crossed over the street and was actually in a queue when she remembered that she only had her bus fare. The change left from Simon wouldn't even buy a cup of coffee.

For the first time ever, there was no one Emma knew in McDonald's, either side of the counter. She settled herself in a corner and read one of their free newspapers until the sweeper-up began giving her area rather more attention than it strictly warranted. Next minute he would be bringing the manager over. Time to leave.

Outside it was dark and still pouring. Emma leaned against the bus stop; the rain was bouncing off the shiny black road surface. She closed her eyes. Her cardigan was sodden, her hair plastered flat to her head. Raindrops coursed like tears down her face and dripped off her chin.

The driver of the car, parked directly across from the bus stop, had been waiting for her. The headlights flared, turning the rain to rods of gold, the twin beams picked her out like a spotlight. The car pulled out, wheels swishing through the puddles and executed a wide U-turn, then it slowed, brake lights glowing bright as it came towards her. His hand was on the passenger door, about to swing it open; the words were forming in his mouth, ready to invite her in. Then a woman stepped out from the shadows. He whispered expletives as Emma turned towards her.

"Emma, is that you? You're soaking! Come on. Quick. You'd better come with me."

The girl turned to greet the woman by her side. Neither of them looked as the car accelerated away.

His hands gripped the steering wheel and he swore again as he nearly collided with a passing car. He'd lost his chance. They were only schoolgirls but they always seemed one step ahead. How did they manage it? Still, there were two of them. Missing one made him all the more determined to get the other. She was the one, after all. She was at the bottom of it.

Out of town, the new bypass meant he could put his foot down. It wasn't far, but he'd better concentrate. The rain, and the new road layout, made the turning for Coombe Ashleigh easy to miss.

Chapter 26

Jude struggled up the hill through the rain and the wind, her light hardly penetrating the darkness in front of her. She changed the Derailleur on her bike down to the lowest gear. Nearly there. Soon the hill would start to flatten out. Ben's house was next on the left. She could see the lights through the trees.

Usually, she liked it when her parents went out, but this evening she'd been unable to settle to anything and had prowled round the house, the evening stretching out, endless hours of boredom. She'd been thinking about Ben and suddenly she had to see him. He would be alone, his folks had gone to dinner somewhere leaving him to look after his little brother.

Back in the kitchen, scrawling "Gone up to Ben's – baby sitting" in marker pen on the white board, it had seemed absolutely the right thing to do, but now she was nearly there, her heart beat fast. She could hardly believe she was doing this.

What was she going to say? I was out for a spin on my bike, in the dark, in the pouring rain, and just happened to ride past your house – hope you don't mind me dropping in? Hardly convincing. The best thing to do was let things take their course and leave out the excuses.

*

David Wyatt missed her by minutes. The house was in darkness, it was quite clear that there was nobody in. He made his way to the rear. In doing so, he tripped the device that turned on the safety light.

He peered in through the kitchen window and then turned to go. The high-powered halogen of the security lamp made it easy to read Jude's message.

"Hi! What are you doing here?"

At the delight on Ben's face and the warmth of his embrace all Jude's doubts about going to see him left her.

"Come in. Get your coat off." He shook the rain from her jacket and hung it up with the higgledy-piggledy assortment of family macs and anoraks which filled up the porch. "I've just got a great big fire going. I'll make some coffee. You go and get warm."

Jude pulled off her boots and padded across the polished wooden floor in her socks. The old half-timbered house had been opened out with one room going into another. The large log fire in the living room gave out a welcome heat and she stood in front of it, admiring the strange and rich collection of furniture, objects, rugs, pictures and wall hangings which adorned the room.

Ben came back, balancing a tray of coffee and biscuits.

"Weird, isn't it?" he commented as he saw her looking round. "Mum says we might as well be living in the warehouse." He put the tray down. "Mostly stuff Dad either can't shift or he's hanging on to, hoping it'll go up in value. Best not to get too comfortable, or too fond of something." He threw himself down into a wide armchair next to the fireplace. "He'll sell anything out from under you if he thinks he's found a buyer."

161

Jude picked up a mug and wrapped her hands round it, absorbing the warmth.

"Who did that?"

Jude indicated an exquisitely worked sampler, up above the fireplace. It carried the message, JUNK'S BEEN GOOD TO ME, surrounded by little embroidered pictures. There was a van with COOPER'S on the side in tiny letters, different pieces of furniture, chairs, a table, a Welsh dresser, a grandfather clock; at the bottom was the front of the antique shop.

"Stevie. Dad's always saying that. It's like, his motto. So Stevie gave him that last Christmas – kind of a joke."

She sat by him, on the floor, resting her head on his knees.

"So?" he asked after a minute or so. "What are you doing here?" He laughed and touched her hair. "What was the matter? Couldn't stay away from me a minute longer?"

"No. Well, yes. Something like that. Now I'm here, though, I feel kind of silly."

"I'm glad you came. Silly or not."

"Umm, so am I . . ." She relaxed against his legs and closed her eyes.

"I asked you if you wanted to come back, this afternoon when we went to the shop, and you turned me down flat."

Jude looked at him and smiled.

"Sometimes," she said, "I have trouble making up my mind."

Jude and Ben had gone down to Cooper's Antiques after school, armed with the photograph, to see if Stevie, Jed Cooper's partner, could identify the beads that were clearly shown round Jenny Beresford's neck and resting on the square-cut low front of her dress.

Stevie was a compact, muscular young woman in T-shirt and dungarees; a rose tattoo showed just below the sleeve on her right shoulder. Jude had met her before on previous visits to Cooper's Antiques because Stevie specialized in clothing and jewellery. They explained what they wanted. Stevie brushed wisps of short spiky blond hair out of her eyes and studied the beads in the photo carefully. Then she began hauling out ledgers from under the counter.

"Sounds like a house clearance," she said, fiddling with the gold earring she wore in her left ear. "I mean, people don't come in off the street with a handful of beads, do they? I don't remember them specifically," she added, throwing the big books open, "but then I wouldn't if they were in with a load of other stuff. I don't comb through everything," she grinned, "got to leave something for the Jude Hughes's of this world to get excited about."

"Look for Wyatt," Ben suggested, "it might save time."

Jude leaned on the counter, looking round, remembering the Saturday she'd come in here, how thrilled she had been. Part of her now wished she'd lobbed the beads right back into the button bowl where she'd found them.

"Yeah. Knew it was in somewhere. And here it is."

Jude and Ben bent over to where she was pointing in the ledger with a nicotine-stained fingernail.

WYATT, DAVID – House Clearance
                            Elm Cottage,
                            Mitre Hill,
                            Coombe Ashleigh

CONTENTS
Furniture:

Below this ran a list of articles and what Cooper's had paid for them.

Ben read out the date. "That's before Christmas."

"So what?" Stevie shrugged and started to roll a cigarette. "Stuff can hang around the shop for ages."

"There's no mention . . ." Jude started to say.

"Wouldn't be," Stevie licked the paper, "probably put down as something like . . . Hang on a minute!" She stuck the finished roll-up behind her ear and hopped off the counter. "I do remember! They were in a tobacco tin. Quite rare and brilliant condition. I know this dealer in London who always gives a good price for them. I put the beads in with the odds and ends and flogged the tin!"

"Thanks, Stevie!" Ben leaned over and kissed her. "I owe you a pint for this!"

"Did you tell Emma?" Ben asked again. Jude seemed to have gone off into a dream. "Did you tell Emma about our great discovery?"

"She wasn't in. I could phone her now, I suppose," Jude said, looking round, "but I don't really want to, I'm much too comfortable. Let's talk about something else. I could do with a change of subject."

"Like what?"

"I don't know . . ." She turned to look at him. "What were you doing before I came, for example?"

"I was trying out a song on the guitar. Trying to get the chords right."

"Carry on, then." She stretched out her legs and leant back against the side of his chair. 'I'll just sit and listen."

"Oh, no. Hey! I'm not very good . . . I couldn't."

"Yes, you could. For me. Please, Ben. Play something."

"Oh, OK. It's Beatles, though." He reached for the guitar, propped up against the side of the mantelpiece, and started tuning it. "I thought you couldn't stand their music."

Jude closed her eyes. "Tell you afterwards. I might be converted."

"Do you know the words?" Jude asked after he had finished.

"Of course I do."

"Then sing it."

"Just for you?"

Jude smiled into the fire. "Yes, just for me."

Ben put the guitar aside. Jude's head was heavy against his legs, her golden hair spilling over his knees.

"Jude? Are you asleep?" he said gently, touching her shoulder.

Her blue eyes opened, close to his. Her skin was warm, rosy from the fire. She smiled sleepily up at him and shook her head. He leant over and kissed her. She turned and put her arms round his neck. Her mouth opened to his as she stroked the short dark hair on the back of his head. Her eyes were closed, long lashes, dark gold, shadowed her cheeks. She was so beautiful.

He gently pulled away and helped her to her feet.

"Shall we go to my room?" he whispered. "We would be more comfortable."

"OK," she said quietly. "But what about your parents?"

He gently tucked a lock of hair behind her ear and traced a finger down the line of her jaw to the cleft in her chin.

"Don't worry about them. They're going on to a club. They won't be back for ages."

"What about your brother."

"Sleeps like a little log." He tipped her face up to his and kissed her again. "He's out for the count. I checked just before you came. Come on . . ."

He held her more tightly, pressing her to him. For a moment she returned the strength of his embrace and then the arm round his back went slack. She braced her hand against his chest and looked down. Her fingers began to trace intricate patterns on the front of his shirt.

"Hey." He ducked down to see her face. "Only if you're sure. If it's what you want. I – I'm sorry, Jude. I didn't mean to pressure you . . ."

"It's not that. I am sure. It is what I want . . ."

"What then? I'll be careful . . ."

She shook her head. "It's not that either."

"What is it, Jude?" His grey eyes locked on to hers and held them. "Is it something I've done? Said? You've got to tell me."

"Nothing like that." Jude smiled and shook her head. "It's nothing to do with you. It's me. I am sure, Ben. Really sure. Let's go to bed, shall we?"

The car was tucked so far under the stand of trees opposite, it hardly showed in the lights of passing traffic. But he had a good view of the house. A thin smile played on his lips as he noted the brief silhouette on the upstairs blind. Anyone seeing a parked car in their headlights on this road, at this time of night, would automatically assume that it contained a courting couple.

He scrunched down into the driver's seat, listening to

the rain drumming on the roof. He reached in his pocket for his flask and twisted off the top. He would be safe enough waiting for her here and then he would be able to do what he liked. After all, baby-sitters can't leave the house and nice girls don't stay all night.

Chapter 27

Jude woke suddenly to a strange room in darkness and the shock of a bare shoulder touching hers. God, they'd gone to sleep! What time was it? She reached for the small digital alarm on the bedside table. Nearly midnight! She sat on the side of the bed, trying to think, trying to clear her head. She had to go. She had to get home, her parents would blow an absolute fuse if she left it any later. As if on cue, from downstairs came the distant ring of the telephone. That was probably them, checking up on her.

"Ben, Ben!" She shook him, urgently whispering, "I've got to go."

"What?" He rolled over and sat up, half asleep, confused to see her there, then he smiled. "Don't go. Come here. Stay for a minute."

"No," she stood up and started hunting down her clothes, "I've got to go. Right now."

She looked at him. Stubble shadowed his face. She put a hand up to her own cheek, the skin still felt tender. Their eyes met.

"It's not because of . . ." he started to say.

She smiled and shook her head. No, that had been fine. Although she did not quite know what to think about it yet. It was not exactly what she'd been led to expect.

He smiled in relief.

She bent over and kissed him on the mouth. Then touched a finger to his lips, forbidding him to speak.

"I have to go. That's all. I'll let myself out."

"Are you sure you'll be OK?" He started to get out of bed. "Hang on a minute. I'll just grab some clothes. I'm coming with you."

"Stay where you are. I'll be fine." She went over to the window and peered out. "It's stopped raining and it's only down the hill. Anyway, you can't leave Michael."

"Oh, all right," he said reluctantly. "But phone me as soon as you get home. Promise."

She turned as she got to the door. "I promise."

It was very dark. No moon or stars. It was freezing, too, with a piercing wind and water-drips from the overhanging trees splashed cold on her head and neck.

Still, it was free-wheeling most of the way home. In the quiet, somewhere near the top of the hill, an engine started. She became aware of a car, coming up behind, and wondered vaguely why the driver was making no attempt to pass her. The road was narrow and curved to the right, with trees growing down either side, but at this time of night there was not much danger of meeting oncoming traffic.

He waited until the point of the bend and then accelerated. His front nearside clipped her back wheel and pitched her violently off the road, into a deep ditch.

Jude lay for a moment, stunned. She'd hit her head on something on the way down and had fallen awkwardly. Her left leg felt numb and there was a sharp pain in her side, like stitch but worse than that. She tried to move but fell back, beginning to black out.

169

It could have been seconds or hours before she opened her eyes again and found herself staring up at high branches of trees. In some distant part of her brain, a voice was reciting the seriousness of her predicament. This was a relatively lonely road, at night there was little traffic. Even if something did pass, down here, they were unlikely to see her. She could be here until morning. And it was wet. The bottom of the ditch contained at least a couple of inches of water and mud. She could feel it soaking through her jacket.

She looked around but could see no significant hand-holds, no good way of pulling herself up. And then she heard it, a car engine whining in reverse. Whoever hit her must have realized and decided to come back. It was like the sound of a prayer being answered.

She called out as soon as she saw the pencil beam coming towards her. She could not see the face behind the torchlight, but she knew the voice. The hand that reached down to help her up belonged to David Wyatt.

Chapter 28

"Phone. Emma," her mother said, "could you get it?"

Emma stood up. Ever since Clare brought her home, they had been round the kitchen table, drinking wine, reminiscing, telling stories. That is, Clare and her mum had. Alison Wyatt just watched, the wine in her glass hardly touched. Emma hadn't said much either. She'd tried not to let it, but the older woman's journalistic fame, her obvious style and wealth, made her feel tongue-tied, self-conscious.

Something else about Alison added to Emma's discomfort. She had an absent quality. When she did answer, it was as though she'd been recalled from far away, and her china-blue eyes took a long time to focus. Emma was beginning to seriously wonder if she might be on something. It was very unnerving.

"Say again?"

Emma held the phone closer and put her hand over her ear.

"Oh, hi, Ben. Sorry. It's just Clare's here with a friend . . . Clare Conrad, yes. Talking over old times with Mum – getting a bit raucous."

Emma tried to listen through the laughter and chatter going on round the kitchen table. Ben's voice sounded strained and urgent.

"Jude? No. Why? Should she be?"

" – *How* long ago?"

Her face became serious and her voice lost its lightness.
"Well, she's not here . . ."

She nodded, " – Yes, that's a good idea . . . Yeah," she nodded again, " – go and have a quick look now if you're worried. And ring me back, will you? Yeah, you too. See you."

Emma returned to Clare saying for at least the tenth time, "Goodness, have you seen the clock? We really must be going."

At the look on Emma's face she broke off.

"Who was that, love?" her mother asked, equally disquieted.

"It was Ben. Asking if Jude was here. Her parents phoned him – she was baby-sitting up at his house and I guess they thought it was getting a bit late – but she left there over half an hour ago . . ."

It was a journey of just a few minutes. Emma bit her lip, unwilling to say out loud what they must be thinking.

"Excuse me, but who's Jude?" Alison asked.

"Oh, sorry," Clare said. "A friend of Emma's and one of my students. Her boyfriend, Ben, is Jed Cooper's kid. Do you remember Jed?"

"Yes. He was a friend of Robbie's. The Coopers still live up the top of the hill?"

"Yes. Same place."

"That's minutes away. Maybe we should go out and have a look for her."

Just then the telephone rang, it was Ben back again. Emma relayed the message to those listening round the table.

"He's found her bike. One wheel's all buckled. Looks like she was involved in some kind of accident. But there's no sign of her . . . No . . ." Clare was indicating for her to

172

hand over the phone. "Ben, don't go. Clare wants to speak to you. Hang on a minute."

"Ben? It's me. Clare. Phone Jude's parents – tell them what you've just told Emma – tell them to phone the police. She could be hurt. She could have wandered off. All right, all right, we'll meet you outside . . ."

"She'd have to be a squirrel to get through that lot."

They were standing at the point where Jude's bike had left the road. It was still there and clearly, from the damage, Jude had been hit by another vehicle. Clare shone the powerful torch slowly up and down the ditch. No sign of her. Above them was what appeared to be impenetrable thicket.

"She's not on the road going up and she's not on the road going down." Clare flicked her torch off. "There's only one other way she could have gone."

"On to the hill," Ali said, thoughtfully.

"It's logical. It is the next turning."

"Unless . . ." Emma started to say.

"Unless what?"

"Unless someone took her away in a car or something."

"Don't be silly, Emma." Fear made Clare's voice schoolma'amish, severe. "Jude wouldn't get in a car with anyone she didn't know. She's far too sensible."

"What if . . . What if she got in the car because she did know the person?"

"I don't get what you mean . . ."

There was nothing for it. Jude could be in terrible danger. Emma found herself spilling it all: beads, photographs, Mrs Stanley's stories, everything. Alison might be angry, embarrassed, but it could not be helped. Emma stammered out their suspicions about her brother as well.

Ben listened and then added that they were definitely the same beads. They had come from the Wyatts' house, Stevie had confirmed it.

Clare said nothing; her puzzlement turned to grim concern as she listened. Alison remained silent until they had finished, and then she looked around. It was as if she was finally waking up. She turned on her heel and started to run.

"Ben," she shouted over her shoulder, "go back and phone the police. Tell them we've gone to my mother's cottage."

Chapter 29

"David – let me in. It's me. Alison." She hammered on the door. Flakes of paint fell off under her assault, exposing bare wood and the green cracked surface she remembered from childhood. "David! I know you're in there. Let me in!"

"The door is open."

Alison leant nearer, listening. The words were echoing and indistinct, as if from inside a tomb.

"What? I can't hear you."

"I said the door's open. You can come in if you want to."

Alison tried the handle. The door creaked slightly and swung inward before sticking on the uneven flagged floor. She cautiously edged round it and entered the dark passageway, motioning for Clare and Emma to stay outside.

They stood undecided for a moment, and then Emma whispered fiercely.

"I'm going in too."

Emma stepped towards the door.

"I don't think we should,' Clare whispered back, catching hold of her arm.

"I reckon he's got Jude," Emma hissed, trying to shake her off.

"How do you know?"

"Call it a feeling, and if he has . . ." Emma wrenched her arm away and moved forward.

"What are you going to do? If he has it's all the more reason to stay out of it." Clare grabbed Emma's coat and forcibly held her back. "Let Alison handle it. We don't know what sort of state he's in or what he's done."

Jude lay, unmoving, on a rumpled khaki sleeping bag in the corner of what had once been the Wyatts' living room. Her eyes were closed. Near her a butane camping lamp hissed and sputtered. In its steady white light Alison could see a gash on her right temple and the beginnings of a large swelling. Purple bruising was already beginning to show against her extreme pallor and the blond hair on that side of her head was matted with drying blood.

"I haven't touched her." David's voice came from the shadows of the deep chimney alcove, next to the girl. "I haven't done anything to her. She did that falling off her bike. She passed out when I got her here."

"She's hurt, David." Alison started across the room towards her.

"Stay there! Stay where you are!" David stood up and moved nearer the sleeping bag. "She's staying here."

"She might be concussed. We have to get her to hospital. It's over, David . . ."

"I will hurt her if you come any nearer. No one's going anywhere!"

They stared at each other. Alison's heart lurched and ice-cold fear trickled through her. He was carrying her father's shotgun. She ordered herself not to show any emotion. She had to stay calm, assess the situation. How to get the girl out, how best to handle David.

That look in the eyes, she'd seen it before. At border crossings and checkpoints, green lines and vehicle searches all over the world, she'd heard that panicky note in the voice, watched the jerking, nervous body movements. Right now, her brother was like all the irregular soldiers she'd ever met. The jittery young boys and solemn, anxious middle-aged men. Erstwhile civilians, unused to carrying guns, itchy fingers on the trigger. Ready to kill anyone – she'd seen them do it.

"What was that?"

They both turned at a faint sound from outside. Alison knew what it was immediately. She had heard it all through her childhood. The back door scraping on the floor.

"Who's there?" David demanded, his voice raising. "Is there somebody with you? Tell them to come in here, right now – or I will hurt her. I mean it, Ali."

"I think she's all right but getting her out won't be easy. He's got a gun." She held up her hand to silence Clare. "You must come in because he knows you are here. But try not to react in any way to anything you see or hear. Leave all the talking to me. You must not do or say anything. No sudden moves. Is that clear?"

Ali's voice was low but wholly commanding. Clare and Emma followed her obediently.

When they entered the room he was sitting on a folding chair next to the makeshift bed, the shotgun across his knees. Emma thought he was asleep, then he looked up. His eyes glittered in the flickering light.

On the sleeping bag, Jude stirred and groaned.

"David?" Alison spoke in the same tone of quiet

authority she had used outside in the corridor. "I would like you to let Clare have a look at Jude. Would that be all right?"

He stared at Clare as though he'd never seen her before but he nodded.

It seemed to take an age for Clare to get across the room. She knelt down next to Jude and felt her pulse. It was good and strong and her eyes were fluttering open, she was coming round.

"May I use . . ."

Clare tried to speak but her throat was dry with fear, the words would not come out. She pointed towards a half-full bottle of mineral water.

He kicked it over to her. She dampened a corner of the sleeping bag and used it to bathe the girl's face, gently swabbing away the dried blood, applying it like a compress to her bruised temple. The cold water was helping to revive her. Jude's eyes opened fully and stared into Clare's in utter bewilderment.

Clare sat Jude up, putting an arm round her to support her. Jude groaned again when Clare touched her ribs.

"Are you OK?" Clare asked.

Jude nodded. "My head and my side hurt."

"Try some of this. It's water, just a little sip. That's it. Now some more."

"How is she?" David asked.

"She's alive – but she needs medical help. Urgently."

David shrugged, suddenly indifferent.

Clare sat back against the wall, cradling the girl to her.

It was probably only seconds ticking by but the silence seemed to stretch into hours. Emma thought she might pass out herself, the tension in the room was so great, but Alison had taken hold of her hand. She could feel the fingers gripping hers now, willing her to keep strong, giving some of her own strength to get Emma through this ordeal. Then the hand slipped out of hers and Alison was on the move, gliding across the room towards her brother.

"David," she was saying. "I want you to give me the gun."

His hand clutched the polished wooden stock convulsively.

"Listen to me," she continued, calm, quiet, hypnotic. "This is only making matters worse, much worse. There's no need for this. I know what happened. I remember. I remember everything. If it has to come out – so be it. It's time. I don't want it hidden any more. And it's my choice, not yours. I'm a grown woman now. So give me that gun." She held her hand out, she was in front of him now. "I'm going to tell them, David."

David Wyatt moved his head. Clare flinched and had to turn away from the private agony contorting his face as he looked up at his sister. Then he reached down to his lap. Nobody breathed as he handed the shotgun over.

Alison took it from him quickly, broke it across her knee, tipped out the cartridges and put them in her pocket. She snapped the barrel closed and placed the gun carefully against the wall behind her.

Far in the distance, the thin wail of a siren came to them through the silence. Alison went over to Jude and knelt down.

"Before they come, before they get here, there is something you must know." Her voice was fierce and urgent.

"About the day Jenny Beresford died. There's something I have to tell you."

Alison's delivery was rapid, unfaltering, given added urgency by the approaching siren. A car screeched to a halt outside but the shouts and rapid footsteps were drowned out by a much nearer sound. Emma had never heard a man sobbing like that; it seemed to wrench and tear at the air around her.

Chapter 30

Simon looked round sternly from where he was shelving returns. He objected to members of the public tapping him on the shoulder. His expression changed when he saw it was Emma. He had been dreading this. Their fractured encounter, yesterday in the café, was still fresh and painful. God knows what she thought about how he had behaved. He had no idea what he was going to say, but he certainly owed her an explanation.

"What are you doing here at this time?" He dumped the books and took her over to the biography section. "Shouldn't you be at school or something?"

Emma folded her arms and looked along the spines on the shelves. Intervening events had rather erased it from her mind, but seeing him like this brought their last meeting back with an uncomfortable jolt and she rather regretted consenting to carry out this particular errand.

"Yes," she said eventually, "but Jude's in hospital. I've just been to see her."

"What's the matter with her?"

"She was involved in an accident. But she's not seriously hurt. Cuts and bruises, mostly. A couple of cracked ribs. She had a bang on the head so they are keeping her in for observation."

"When did this happen?"

"Last night." Emma took his arm. "She fell off her

bike. I'll tell you about it on the way. You've got to come with me."

"What, now? I can't. I . . ."

"You've got to," Emma insisted. "Tell them it's an emergency. Tell them it's to do with your sister."

They were heading down towards the river. Although the day was mild, it always seemed colder there than anywhere else. Simon began to wish he had not left his coat in the library.

"Where are we going?" he asked Emma again.

"You'll see when we get there," she replied.

He'd asked her several times but she still wasn't telling. They lapsed into silence. After a brief outline of what had happened to Jude, Emma had become uncharacteristically monosyllabic, refusing point-blank to explain where they were going. He told her he found all this mystery absolutely infuriating, and childish, but even that got no reaction. Finally he gave up. They walked along, side by side, in silence.

Emma turned off the road and he followed her into the forecourt of a block of flats. She pressed one of the buttons on the wall next to the entrance. Presently, a distorted voice answered. Emma pushed the glass door open as someone buzzed them up.

He followed her into the lift. It stopped at the second floor.

Emma led him to the second flat along the corridor and rang the bell.

The door opened and there she was. Simon suddenly found it hard to breathe. He tried not to stare. He would have known her anywhere: the short red hair, the delicate, rather patrician features, the startling eyes, china blue, against ivory-pale skin.

"Hello. Simon, isn't it? Emma's told me all about you. It's good of you to come," she said. "I'm . . ."

"I know," he interrupted, shaking her hand. "Alison Wyatt. I recognize you from the television. And from . . ."

He could see the resemblance now. It was in the eyes. The woman had the same gaze as the arrogant tomboy child. A look that went into you and through at the same time, challenging and dismissing at a single glance.

"Yes. I was with Jenny, in the photo you lent to Emma. Come in."

He followed her into a spacious living room overlooking the river.

"Nice view."

"It's my friend Clare's flat. That's why she chose it."

"Clare?"

"Conrad. She teaches Emma."

"Yes, I know . . ." He glanced at his watch. "Look, I should be at work . . ."

"Clare was also with Jenny. We were the last people to see her alive. Sit down." It was not a request, or even an invitation. "I'm sure they can spare you for half an hour. I have something to tell you. It concerns your sister, Jennifer. By the way, I don't think you've met my brother. David, come and meet Simon."

He was out on the balcony. Simon recognized him from the bar in the hotel. His acquiline features were accentuated by his drawn face and his skin had a greyish tinge, like someone who has suffered a long illness; but seeing them together, it was possible to tell they were brother and sister.

There was something else. Simon watched them as

Emma came in with the coffee. It was as if some deep connection running between them had been broken and recently renewed. Like on those TV programmes where people were united after many years apart. They couldn't stop looking at each other.

"Simon?"

Alison put down her coffee cup and folded her hands on her lap. He was about to hear what this was all about. He could not guess what was coming, but something about her sudden formality chilled him. His hand shook a little as he picked up his cup. A feeling both irrational and absurd swept through him. A desire to go, leave right now. A sense of emptiness, of being bereft. What did one do at the end of a quest?

"David and I have asked you here because we want you to know exactly what happened to your sister. No, don't say anything. Just listen."

Only the slightest tremor in her voice betrayed her nervousness.

"I'll tell him if you like," David muttered.

"No." Alison shook her head. "I have to do it. Simon, I killed your sister . . ."

Emma sat and listened again to the story she'd heard hurriedly told the night before. She watched Simon's face, saw the horror register there, saw him lean forward in his chair, eyes fixed on Alison, avid for every detail. Told like this in daylight, in the quiet of Clare's living room, it sounded worse, more graphic.

"It was an accident," Alison was saying. "We were playing, just Jenny and me, in my dad's allotment shed. We weren't supposed to be there – I'd been told to keep

184

out of there so many times, but that just made it more exciting. First we played hippies – that's how she had those marks on her face. We picked flowers – sweet williams – and I decorated each cheek with a lipstick I'd swiped from a stall at the fête and wrote LOVE across her forehead.

"We were playing *Top of the Pops*. We . . . we climbed up on the workbench to dance, using it like a stage. She had the beads. She was throwing them round her neck, swinging them about. She'd promised to let me wear them – it was a trade for letting her play in our shed – but then she wouldn't let me have them. Jenny could be like that, nice one minute, then she'd go back on her word, start taunting you. I was so angry. She'd promised . . ." Alison's hands tensed. "She swung them up right into my face and I got really furious. I grabbed them and started twisting, turning them round and round. Until she started to choke. She pulled away, I don't know . . . Anyway, the string broke. The beads scattered, bouncing all over the place, and Jenny fell backwards off the bench. She fell back . . ." Alison paused and passed a hand over her face, holding it over her mouth for a second before going on.

"At the end of the bench there was a vice holding the handle of a large sickle, it was almost as big as a scythe. Dad used it for corners and long grass, he was splicing on a new handle or something. Anyway, the blade was on the floor, sticking up, and – when Jenny fell – it went through her. She just lay there looking up. Never moved. Never closed her eyes. She must have died instantly. I don't know what I did after that. The next thing I remember was David coming."

"I was looking for Dad," David said quietly, "he was supposed to be down on the allotment. I couldn't see him working so I had a look in the shed. And I found Ali. Just sitting in a corner, staring. I told her to go, not to tell anyone, and then I hid the sickle and . . . and Jenny's body."

"Why?" Simon asked at last. "If it was an accident. Why did you hide it?"

"At first – it didn't occur to me that Ali had done it. God forgive me. I thought it might have been my old man or . . . or Robbie."

"How did you know it wasn't?"

"At first she wouldn't speak, wouldn't say a thing. Then a few words stumbled out, enough to piece together what must have happened. And the beads. When I got home she still had some of them in her hand. The rest were in her pocket. Then Mum took over. She said, if I thought it was Dad or Robbie, what would the police think? And if we told them it was Ali – they probably wouldn't believe us anyway and if they did, they'd take her away. Ma never trusted the authorities. If they don't get you for one thing, they'll get you for another – that's what she used to say. Anyway, she made me and Robbie go out later that night and clean up as best we could and . . . and get rid of the body."

"Is that when you met Eileen Stanley?" Emma asked suddenly.

"Yes." David looked surprised. "How did you know about that? When we met her, I was really panicking. But when I told Mum, she just said, 'Eileen's a good girl. She won't tell nobody.' And she didn't. Neither did anybody else."

"Why not?" Simon asked. "I mean, the death of a child . . . Surely . . ."

"Most people from the village believed a stranger did

it. Those that knew different had their own reasons for keeping quiet."

For a moment or two nobody spoke. Simon stared down. He concentrated on a section of pattern on the Persian rug, acutely aware of them watching, waiting for his response. He was finding it hard to control the sudden rage sweeping through him at the way these people had orchestrated this. They had it all worked out even now. Christ! Even Emma was in on it.

There was only one question Simon wanted to ask, but he had to get a hold of himself first before he could ask it.

"What . . . ," his voice sounded strange. He tried again. "What do you intend to do?"

David Wyatt started to speak and then deferred to his sister.

"Obviously we must hand the matter over to the police. David, we must," she said as her brother tried to interrupt. "It's what we agreed. There has been so much damage done, to us, to everyone. It's time it all came out. Out into the open."

David Wyatt's shoulders sagged as he reached down into his pocket and took out Jude's beads.

"And we are going to take them these."

"May I see?"

Simon's hand was already extended to accept the necklace. He examined it carefully, picking out the beads that had belonged to Jennifer, his sister.

"We could not go before we told you," Alison was saying, "and . . . and we'd like you to come with us."

"What for?" Simon's voice was sullen, sarcastic, heavy with anger. "As some sort of witness? To watch you unburden your guilt? Or do you want me to act as Jennifer's representative and hand out my forgiveness?"

David moved protectively towards his sister, alerted by the aggression in the other man's voice, but Ali's face registered only slight surprise. She continued to regard Simon steadily, absorbing his anger, taking it into her.

"It's your decision," she said quietly.

Simon stared back, his flaring rage replaced by a curious calm spreading through him. Despite his outward appearance, he'd felt nervous when he got here; having no idea how to react to what he would hear, or how he would feel once he knew. Anger, of course. Grief, too. For his mother and her love for her lost dead child, the sister he never knew. Such feelings were predictable, but this was something new. He would make Alison Wyatt wait for his answer until he had had time to examine the idea forming in his head, clear and hard, crystallized from hatred.

He looked down at the beads, pooled in the palm of his hand.

"I'm keeping these. You're not having them back, even to hand over to the police. Especially not to hand over to the police. That would be too neat and tidy."

"What do you mean?" Ali asked.

"After all this time, what are they going to do? When it happened, how old were you? Seven, eight? A child – below the age of prosecution. They'll close the file. Personally, I'd call that letting you off lightly, very lightly. No." He leant towards her, his mouth curving up into a vindictive smile. "My mother's sanity hangs by a thread as it is. I don't want her knowing about this. So you'll just have to carry on living with it, won't you!"

"If you want to hurt me," Ali said evenly, "I can tell you a much better way. I am moderately well-known, a media personality. For people like me, fame can just as quickly turn to notoriety. Just call the tabloids, they'd love to hear all about my part in the Beresford case, probably even pay you. Here," she reached in her bag and handed him a card, "phone this number . . ."

"Don't bother." Simon stood up to go. "Like I said, that's too clean and easy. I want it slow. You can destroy yourself far more effectively."

He turned and walked towards the door.

"Wait!" Alison Wyatt's clear command stopped him half-way across the room. "Simon. Have you considered, I mean, really considered your mother? I suggest you stop behaving like a child and come back here."

Simon's fair skin turned a dull red, it even spread to the back of his neck. By his side, his fist clenched and unclenched as he countered Alison's calm cool stare and Emma thought for a moment that he might be going to hit her.

"What do you mean?" Simon enunciated each word carefully, as though his mouth was affected by an oral anaesthetic.

"I mean how much have you thought about your mother?"

"What kind of question is that? Of course I've thought about her! Now listen . . ."

"No. You listen to me." Ali's clear voice took on further authority. "I think you are being arrogant and selfish. Who are you to choose what your mother does or does not know, what she does or does not hear?"

"Ever since before I was born she's been in and out of mental hospital. I have to protect her."

"Because of what happened to Jenny, yes?"

"Because of what you did to her."

"Don't be so petulant and vindictive, Simon," Ali said,

189

leaning towards him. He began to say something. She held up a slim ringed hand to silence him. "No. Let me speak. I know something, a small part, of what your mother has gone through. It's only recently, very recently, that I've been able to recall these events to my conscious mind, but I have not gone unscathed, whatever you might think. And – I want you to think about this. Wouldn't it be better, for your mother, whatever her state of health, to know that Jenny's death was a terrible accident and not the result of some evil intent? That she died instantly and she did not suffer? There has been talk over the years of ritual murder, satanic abuse, and I don't know what, because of the marks on her face and all that witchcraft rubbish. Your mother must have gone through agonies, imagining Jenny in pain, frightened and alone, among sadistic strangers. What kind of son are you? You have the chance to rid her of all that, put her mind at rest, and you won't take it."

Simon stared, his features set as though carved from stone. Ali carried on, relentless.

"Too many people know. I can't keep this quiet, Simon. Even for you, even if I wanted to. It's news, and news has a way of getting out, no matter how hard you try to stop it. Wouldn't it be better if David and I went with you, to tell your mother ourselves, or would you rather she read about it in the Sunday papers?"

Simon started to speak and then changed his mind. He looked slowly from one to the other, and then giving an odd, curt little nod in the direction of Emma, he left the flat.

Alison sank back in her chair, hands raised helplessly in a gesture of defeat. David Wyatt rose to go after Simon but his sister held on to his arm.

"Let him go," she said, eyes closed, massaging her forehead above the bridge of her nose.

"What are we going to do now?" David asked.

Alison looked at him. Unshed tears intensified the blue of her eyes and her finely shaped mouth tugged down at the corners like a child's.

"Go to the police, of course," she said eventually. "What else is there to do?"

Chapter 31

David and Alison Wyatt dropped Emma off at the hospital on their way to the police station. They hardly spoke after leaving Clare's flat, preoccupied by the heavy task that lay before them and, as the car drove away, neither of them looked back.

Emma bought flowers from the little stall inside the gates and, tucking the mixed bunch under her arm, headed across the car park. It was raining now. Grey clouds hung down over the hospital buildings and drops drummed on to the transparent canopy over the entrance. Emma pushed through the swing doors and looked up at the signs, trying to remember which way to go, then she set off up stairs and along corridors, following the arrows.

The first thing she thought, when she entered was, "Jude's gone". She was staring at the stripped bed, wondering vaguely what she should do with the flowers, when a cheerful young staff nurse came up and redirected her to the patients' day-room.

"Your friend's in there, love," she said, "watching television."

Jude was so deeply engrossed in one of the afternoon soaps, she did not even glance up as Emma came through the door.

Emma stood for a moment, looking round. She could see why there was no one else in there. A set of fire regulations provided the sole wall decoration. Black vinyl wooden-armed chairs faced each other across a large coffee table stained by intricate patterns of overlapping cup rings. The whole place reeked of illicit cigarettes and the only source of entertainment, besides the television, was a dog-eared *Take a Break* magazine and a couple of curled-up copies of *Bella*.

"What a dismal place," she said, dropping into the seat next to Jude. "No wonder they all stay in bed."

"Emma! Sorry, didn't realize it was you. I thought it was a nurse or one of the other patients."

"Well? How are you?"

Jude shifted in her chair and grimaced as pain grabbed at her side and shoulder.

"I'm OK, I suppose. They think so, anyway. They're throwing me out. I've been sent in here to wait. Mum and Dad should be arriving to get me any minute. They've given me painkillers but all along here still feels swollen."

Jude gingerly touched the side of her face. Her left jaw was grazed from chin to ear and purple-grey bruises smudged her cheek. Butterfly stitches showed under the hair falling down over her forehead.

"Do you think it will leave a mark?" Jude said, indicating her temple.

"Shouldn't think so," Emma gently held back a wave of golden hair, "that's why they use those butterfly things. Even if it does . . ." she scrutinized her friend's face, "scars are interesting. Flawed beauty is definitely in. They're painting them on. It's true! I read it in *Elle* or somewhere, just the other week. I'm serious!"

"Emma, don't. Please! I'm all strapped round here." She spread her hand over her ribs. "It really kills me to laugh – feels like I'm breaking apart."

"Sorry. What shall we talk about, then?"

"Something that isn't funny."

"OK . . ." Emma sank back in her chair and stared up at the ceiling. "How about this for not funny."

Jude listened to what had happened at Clare's flat.

"The police have been to see me – about last night," she said when Emma finished.

"When?"

"This morning. He, the policeman, wanted me to go over what happened. He said a couple of things needed clarification."

"Like what?"

"How, exactly, the accident happened for a start-off. I tried my best but I don't think I was much help. I don't remember it very well," she touched the bruising round her temple, "because of the concussion. It's strange. I can recall bits, like being in the ditch and Wyatt helping me up, but not how I got there. Then nothing till I saw Clare, and you were there with Alison Wyatt . . ." Jude frowned, trying to think back intensified her headache. "Then he started going on about time discrepancies and asking me why Wyatt took me to the cottage in the first place."

"What did you say?"

"I said I didn't know – they'd have to ask him."

Emma looked up at the clock. "They won't have to go far. The Wyatts should have arrived at the police station by now. Do you think they'll charge him with anything?"

Jude shrugged. "Have to wait and see. We didn't discuss that. All he said before he left was, 'Next time you go out on your bike, be a good girl and wear a helmet.' "

Emma laughed. "My advice would be don't go on a bike. Full stop."

"Do you think you'll see him again?" Jude asked after a while.

"Who? Wyatt? I guess so. I've got him tomorrow after-noon. Unless he's been arrested."

"No, not him." Jude shook her head. "I meant Simon."

"Oh. I don't know. No, I shouldn't think so."

Emma lapsed into silence and closed her eyes. She was stretched out in the chair, her body still, but the quick movement of her thin nervous hands on the wooden arms betrayed her agitation. Jude did not say anything, either. She knew Emma too well to ask directly what was the matter. Finding out meant knowing when to speak and when to listen.

"You should have seen the look he gave me," Emma said quietly. "I knew what they were going to tell him. I should have warned him. I just didn't think about the effect it would have. I thought about it differently. Like, you know, he'd just find it interesting, solving the case, getting to the bottom of a mystery. It never occurred to me that Alison's story would hurt him so deeply and now he's kind of lumped me in with them. I got it all wrong. Why am I so stupid? What makes me so bloody insen-sitive?"

Jude did not respond but waited for her to carry on. Emma had to discover the answers to the questions she posed herself; her own opinion didn't matter. A little bit of self-analysis might do her good. Pride rarely allowed Emma to admit faults and Jude had never heard her go this far towards confessing that sometimes, in some things, she did lack judgement.

"I just . . . just can't leave it like this. I ought to tell him they're going to the police, apart from anything else . . ." Emma paused, trying to control the uncharacteristic shake in her voice. "I don't know what to do . . ."

"Go and see him," Jude stated decisively. "Talk to him. Tell him what you just told me."

"I don't even know where he is."

"Yes, you do," Jude said, "he'll be in the library."

Emma furled the umbrella, lent to her by Jude's mother, and scanned Issues and Returns. No sign of him. A prowl up and down the ranks of shelves and through the other sections brought her back to the counter. Nothing. Simon was nowhere to be seen.

She was just about to go, when a voice said:

"Need any help? Emma. Emma Tasker, isn't it?" The girl at Enquiries smiled pleasantly. "I'm Monica," she held out the badge on her shirt. "Monica Allenby. Don't you remember?"

Emma did recall her vaguely, from a couple of years ago at school.

"Yes, of course. Hi," she said, approaching the desk, "I'm, er, looking for Simon, actually. Simon Freeman. But I can't see him. You don't happen to know if he's around anywhere, do you?"

"I think he might have left." A look of concern crossed Monica's well-scrubbed, open face. "He had a message this morning, some sort of family bereavement. If you'll hang on a minute, I'll go and see."

She disappeared into the part of the library not open to the general public. Emma picked up a pamphlet about Adult Education courses; none of the information registered as she flicked through the pages. She was halfway through *Guided Country Walks* when someone tapped her on the shoulder.

"Hello," he said, "I understand you wanted to see me."

"Yes. I, er . . ." Emma crumpled the leaflet she was holding and thrust it into her pocket. Now he was here, she didn't know what to say.

"Perhaps you came to apologize," he suggested, arms folded. "Or isn't 'I'm sorry' in your vocabulary?"

She looked up at him, still unable to speak.

He let out a short bitter laugh. "You don't even know why you should, do you? Dragging me to that flat this morning, without any warning or explanation, to confront Alison Wyatt and have her tell me in graphic detail exactly how she killed my sister. Have you any idea how that felt?"

Emma looked away from the pain in his eyes.

"No," Simon went on, "of course not. You don't think much, Emma, do you? About other people, their feelings, the consequences of your actions."

"I do . . ." Emma started to protest.

Simon shook his head. "No, you don't. You . . ."

"I do. Or at least I'm trying to." Emma shook her head, refusing to let him interrupt. Even if he didn't want to hear, he was going to listen. "I'm sorry. I'm really sorry. Think what you like, but one of the reasons I came was to apologize. I didn't realize. I should have told you, but they said not to and . . . and I thought, because it was their story, they should be the ones to say, not me. But that's not the only reason I came." She scanned his face. His expression gave her no help or encouragement. "I thought you ought to know," she continued, "they are going to the police. They're with them right now. And so . . ."

"So what? I knew they'd do that."

"So the story will get out now. And I thought if you knew, you could go and talk to your mother, and warn her so it won't come as a total shock to her if . . . if, like Alison Wyatt says, it gets into the papers."

"How thoughtful of you, Emma." He looked down at her with a thin smile. "Consider everything I've just said taken back."

"All right. If that's how you feel . . ."

There was really nothing more to say. Part of what he had said was justified, and Emma could understand the anger he felt, but there was nothing she could do, apart from apologize, and she'd already done that. As for her other reason for coming here – forget it. She must have been mad even to think of asking him; she flinched at the thought of how he would react.

"I'm off to see my mother now," he said, as she turned to go. "It is going to be in the papers . . ."

"How do you know?"

"I phoned that number she gave me. Got through to one of the tabloids. What do you think the guy said?"

Emma shook her head.

"He said, 'You're too late, mate. The lady herself just phoned in the copy.' What do you make of that?"

Emma shrugged. "I really don't know . . ."

Maybe Alison Wyatt was pre-programmed to self-destruct; maybe it was something she had to do as a kind of therapy. Or it could be part of some long game of her own. Emma could only guess at most what might go on in such a complex, convoluted mind, and at the moment she was all out of guesses.

"Right then," he said, picking up his holdall. "I'm off. I probably won't see you again . . ."

"Simon, wait." Emma took a deep breath and followed him out. It was now or never. "Would you mind . . . Can I come with you to see your mother?"

His eyes widened at her completely unexpected request. He dropped his bag with a bang on the pavement.

"It was something my mum said yesterday. And then today, meeting Jude's mother . . ."

Emma could not explain to him but seeing Mrs Hughes at the hospital had affected her deeply. She looked so much older. Her face was a mask of tension, and there was something, almost a hunger, when she saw Jude, like a fierce cat who's got her kitten back. She was trying hard but each smile was a conscious effort. Her agitated, distracted gaze suggested that it would take time to erase the things she had seen when she thought she had lost her daughter.

"I started thinking about what a terrible time your mother must have had, not just when it happened, but all those years of doubt, of not knowing. I think Alison's right about that. It would be better to know. I'd want to, wouldn't you? And I could help you to tell her. It can help to have another person with you when you have to talk to someone about something as difficult as that . . ."

Emma tailed off. Even in her own ears it sounded insincere. So much babble. She stared at the pavement, unable to find the words for why she wanted to follow the story to its very core; to try to understand the true nature of that terrible event, by having the courage to face the emotional havoc that lay at the centre.

"And sometimes it can't." He finished the sentence for her. "The answer has to be no, Emma. Not because of you, because of her, my mother. She doesn't cope well with strangers around. But," he smiled, "it was kind of you. A kind offer. I – I underestimated you. I read you wrong, and I'm sorry. Look, I have to leave now . . ."

"Well, good luck."

"Thanks. You too." He held her close for a moment before letting her go. "Take care, Emma. Here, you might as well have these." He reached in his pocket and took out the beads.

"Don't you want them?"

He shook his head. "It's going to be hard enough without showing her these. You keep them – as a reminder. Then when you're a hot-shot journalist, maybe you won't forget. Behind every story, there's someone like my mother."